F81

Cyborgs: More Than Machines

By
Eve Langlais

Copyright © April 2012, Eve Langlais
Cover Art by Amanda Kelsey© April 2012
Content Edited by Brandi Buckwine
Produced in Canada

Published by Eve Langlais
Ontario, Canada
www.EveLanglais.com
ISBN-13: 978-1475138733
ISBN-10: 1475138733

Prologue

In my dreams, I have a name. A home. A family and friends. I can even see their faces and hear their voices. Feel their hugs and affection. Bask in the warmth of their love.

In my dreams, I am different, carefree, and happy. I speak when I want to. I feel emotions, a torrent of them, and stranger than that, my body is entirely covered in pink flesh. My hair is long and unbound, silky strands of gold that swirl around me, clinging to my brightly colored garments.

In my dreams, I recall a time when I still know how to sing, laugh, and dance.

In my dreams, I am alive.

I hate waking from my fantasy. Hate losing that thread to my old life, those happier times. But that world is gone now. I am no more. The little part of me that remembers is snuffed out when I wake, like a flame before the breeze. But not completely forgotten, instead, tucked away and hidden in the dark recesses of my mind lest they find it and take it from me.

I am no longer Fiona. I am no longer anyone. Not that I have the capacity to care anymore.

In my dreams, I can recognize my existence is a nightmare, one I will never wake from.

In my dreams, I forget I am not human.

But when I wake, I know exactly what I am. Who I have become. I am an android, unit F814, a worker droid with no past or feelings.

Outside of my dreams, I am but a machine, and I exist to serve humanity.

Chapter One

"Dig faster, you lazy excuse for a droid." The foreman's words hit her along with his sour spittle, so close did he stand while his electric whip danced at his side. The eager sparks of his tool jumped from the coil as if daring her to gainsay him, trying to goad her into asking for a sizzling lick.

She did not respond to the bait, couldn't because her very programming precluded it.

Even if she could, replying would serve no purpose, something she knew from her observations. Responding to taunts didn't, after all, help the humans sent to toil alongside her as punishment. Actually, their outspoken attitudes tended to hamper them, their injuries from the discipline meted often crippling limbs which usually resulted in their termination—because the company didn't pay to upkeep dead weight. Speaking out didn't aid defective droid units who thought to question authority and ended up reprogrammed. To stand against the foreman was to invite discipline, on top of what she already put up with. Besides, the leader of her workgroup always said the same insulting things despite the evidence of her efficiency.

Why he lied, she could not decipher, so she ignored his words, and kept swinging her pick against the veined rock face. Kept working. It was safer that way. Alongside the other mechanical beings, her fleshy droid model was the most susceptible to damage. It made her careful. She always made sure she worked just as quickly as the others, and more effectively. Whereas the other robots swung without a care at the striated stone, she analyzed and chose where to hit. Each strike of her pick loosened large chunks of the precious ore. She knew she gave the best quality and quantity of all the workers. Not that the fat human in charge cared. He just liked to flout his authority. Accusing her of laziness was just what he liked to do to prove he controlled her.

And yet I am stronger than him. A strength bound by her programming—*thou shalt not kill*—and used by the humans overseeing her. The foreman often mocked her because of it—*'Stupid droid. What are you going to do about it?'* Nothing. What a shame.

The foreman enjoyed proving his domination over her and the others. Did it every chance he could, keeping her at his beck and call, forcing her to complete the most inane tasks—*'Fetch me a coffee,' 'Clean my tent,' 'Run around the habitat five times.'* He proved his mastery of her every night and didn't care that she lay still and unresponsive beneath his sweating body. She never let him know she found his touch repulsive, even when he asked her directly. An odd loophole in her programming allowed her to lie. So she did. The truth would serve no purpose, or so her analytical mind surmised. He would just retaliate in some other way.

Her internal dictionary had a word for him: sadist, someone who enjoyed inflicting pain and discomfort on others. He'd order her into a stasis mode, sometimes for days and didn't care that her stomach ached from hunger, and that she froze at night from the cold, unable to regulate her temperature. He liked controlling her, and no matter what degradation he performed, nobody would stop him. She couldn't even stop him. Could do nothing but allow herself to be used despite what her rebellious thoughts screamed—usually kill—because, after all, she wasn't supposed to think.

Obviously she possessed a defect in her programming. A flaw which if discovered would see her sent in for reprogramming or even worse, dismantling as often happened to older, obsolete models. *But I am not old, or am I?* She didn't know for sure. Her memory banks only extended nine months. Two hundred and sixty five days, seven hours, thirty one minutes to be precise. Before that, just a blank existed. She did not recall her birth from the factory, nor even the place of her origin. Her first awakened moment occurred here, on asteroid seventy-four, part of the Eunomia cluster the company claimed rights to and now mined with determination.

She must have fallen into a loop as her mind spun in its familiar patterns and slowed her swinging arm because a sizzling arc of electricity stung her. The coil of the whip wrapped around her fleshy arm and drew forth a gasp as her whole frame trembled from the current passing through her. It stung, the pain a familiar friend which she embraced because it at least stole her, even for just a moment, from the barren, coldness of her existence. But this time, the pain didn't stop.

The vision in her eyes grew dim and her limbs quivered, suddenly weak. Was this the end? Had the foreman finally fried her hardware? She'd never reacted like this in the past to the whip. Never felt all her energy waning as her system shut down. She buckled, falling to her knees, her hearing and sight fading, but not enough to miss the foreman's words.

"Shit. Someone get the general on the line. He's going to want to know about this."

And then nothing.

*

Fight Fiona. Fight damn you. Don't let them do this!
Do what? Who was Fiona? And whose familiar voice did she hear, its echo fading as her brain computer interface came back online? In the midst of a system reboot, she could not prevent herself from hitting the ground face first, her limbs still frozen at her sides. Nor could she spit out the dirt clinging to her lips, grinding against her teeth and gums. Waiting for full mobility to

return, her internal processor ran an analysis on her condition; blood ratio was adequate, heart was functioning at a proper level, auditory and visual receptors booting, nerve and muscle control imminent. Her diagnostic noticed some slight bruising and scrapes, minor matters already being tended by the nanobots in her circulatory system.

Physical status ascertained, she took a moment to decipher her situation. Last she recalled, the foreman caught her with his whip and she executed the human equivalent of a swoon. Inert and useless, had the foremen ordered some bots to remove her from the mine while she recovered?

The heavy breathing from above—a familiar sound, which she discovered in that moment, she truly hated—led her to believe the foreman oversaw her current disabled state. She should let him know that she suffered no lasting effects from the punishment—*except a deep burning inside me that wants to...*

Struggling with the strange sensation inside her, she hesitated to let him know she woke. Something, an illogical sense of something not quite right, held her back.

The discharge from the whip must have rendered me even more defective than before. Had the foreman sensed this? Did he even now prepare to reprogram her, or worse dismantle her for parts? It wouldn't surprise her.

Machines didn't matter to him or anyone else. Robots were expendable. Just look at her. A useless droid, deemed unsuitable for earth-side work, shipped to the outer part of the galaxy to work until her parts could no longer be replaced. She was just an object, owned by the Mintorium Mining Company, expected to do what she was told, without a word of complaint. No matter how unfair. No matter how she grew to hate it. No matter what she felt. Caring, after all, wasn't supposed to be in her programming, and until a month ago, just before her hundred and forty second taste of the whip, it wasn't. She should have reported herself to the tech squad for an in-depth analysis. She chose not to.

Now, one unexpected reboot later, her very first since cognizance, she couldn't stop pondering the odd sensations and musings flooding her synapses. If she didn't know better, she'd think she felt emotions, which seemed improbable. Yet, how else to explain the chaos in her mind? First and foremost—*I don't want to be recycled. It's not fair. He's the one who damaged me.*

The train of thoughts surprised her, the concept of fairness a new one, and she didn't know where it sprang from. But once it attached itself to the logical part of her BCI, it refused to shake free. She pondered its meaning as she lay inert on the ground. Analyzed its definition but couldn't understand how it applied to her. *Robots have no rights. So why is my situation unfair?* She mulled it over and over as the foreman rolled her onto her back, grunting and panting at her weight. As all her systems came back online, she concluded that while she understood the definition, she didn't understand why she felt that way, or even how she knew she felt it. Inanimate objects didn't get a choice when it came to fairness, and they shouldn't care. But, somehow, despite her machine status, she'd discovered a sense of self. How fascinating. What to do about it, though?

"Well, I'd say it was nice knowing you, but I'd be lying. Although, I'll sure miss using your cunt." The crude words of her supervisor only served to increase the burning sensation coursing through her body.

Thoughts still processing the intriguing concept of fairness, she debated whether to keep feigning unconsciousness. Programming dictated she let the foreman know she still functioned—even if she didn't want to. She popped her eyes open to see him straddling her, a gun pointed at her head. This wasn't how termination occurred. Didn't she own a switch like the other units? And what was he doing with a projectile

8

weapon? While some kind of defense was required in the outer reaches because of pirates, guns, with actual bullets, were deemed unsuitable in domed habitats because of the high risk of cracking the shield. Laser pistols were the approved weapon as their searing heat could be absorbed by the domes and rendered harmless.

She almost asked him what he did with an illegal arm and why he thought he could use it to improperly terminate her, but locked her jaw and vocal cords at the last moment. She wasn't programmed to speak aloud unless asked a direct question. And yet…she had to fight not to. To demand what he was doing. Just more evidence her wiring was, as the technicians called it, fried.

"Nothing to say?" The obese human laughed. "I don't see why the general's so worried about you. He sent you out here as some kind of test, supposedly. Told me to work you hard, harder actually than the other drones. He wanted to see if you'd break, and now that you have, he thinks you're a danger. I'm not sure why. You're just a dumb fucking, robot aren't you? Look at you, lying there staring at me even though you know I'm gonna blow your circuits out. Seems like such a fucking waste. But orders are orders." He lowered the weapon until the opening in the barrel rested on her forehead.

One shot, fired this close, and she would be terminated. Even with her nanotechnology, she couldn't recover from a direct wound to her cortex.

"It would be such a shame to kill you, though, before I've had a chance to say goodbye." He pulled back the gun and leered. "What do you say, you pathetic excuse for a bot, to one last hurrah?" With a chuckle, he laid the pistol beside her on the ground and his hands went to the buckle of his trousers.

F814 peered up at the dome overhead which covered the whole mining camp, regulating temperature and air for the living organisms within. Its semi-opaque nature allowed her to almost see the stars. How she would have liked to see them for real, just once, no matter how irrational. How she would have liked to do a lot of things.

And why can't I? Did she need to lie still while the foreman destroyed her? Did she need to senselessly die? Did she dare say no to what the humans demanded?

Looking upon the leering countenance of the corpulent human who'd dropped his pants to reveal his small tool of degradation, she decided, despite all her programming, *I can say no.*

"I do not want to be touched." The words, softly spoken, didn't immediately register with him as he fumbled with her clothes, attempting to tear open the clasps to bare the mammary glands they'd outfitted her with, making her appear female. A waste of tissue on a droid, she personally thought.

"I said that I do not want to be touched, nor do I want to die." She sat up and pushed at his torso, the force of her rejection sending him stumbling back,

Her words got his attention. His eyes went wide. "You can't say no. You're a robot. You'll do what I damn well tell you to."

A twitch in her lips surprised her. Why did they want to curl? "I am a machine. A defective one perhaps, but I still don't want to die."

"Well, that's just too fucking bad," he retorted, but she could see the bead of sweat that rolled down the side of his face. Why did he appear anxious? She saw the flicker of his eyes as he peeked at the gun still on the ground.

He fears me. The knowledge almost froze her. He foolishly moved. A mistake. She propelled herself faster than him, kicking the weapon out of reach before facing him, her lips pulled tight. "I said no." The more she spoke, the more determined the words emerged. To her surprise, the foreman took a step back from her, then another.

Where was the dominant male who ruled with an iron, sweaty fist? Where was the man, who gave orders and punished those who didn't obey? He certainly wasn't in the trembling excuse standing before her with his penile extension shrunk so small as to almost disappear.

"I command you to obey me," he shouted. He added a string of numbers and letters after his request.

She cocked her head and waited. She felt no urge to follow his decree. Nothing changed inside her. No, that wasn't true, the burning sensation that roiled through her body, grew more intense. It demanded action. It wanted…vengeance. She took a step forward, her fingers flexing.

"I've used the code. Now submit, damn you."

"Perhaps you uttered it wrong." She took another step forward, then another.

He stumbled back, his lips moving as he spat more streams of numbers and letters. None stopped her implacable approach, and he finally realized it when he tripped around his own fallen trousers and landed on his posterior. She ended up towering over him, her shadow engulfing his shivering frame.

She could not stop her mouth from curving this time. It must have been quite the frightening look because the foreman blanched and raised his hands defensively.

"I won't kill you," he blubbered. "I promise. Just let me go. I won't tell the general what happened. I won't—"

"No, you won't because I've come up with my own orders." She reached down to grab his tunic and hauled him to his feet. "I've decided that the only one who needs to die is you."

"You won't get away with this," he blustered even as his hands clawed uselessly at her iron grip.

"I already have." In one swift motion, she grabbed his head and twisted, the satisfying snap of bone

11

breaking probably the nicest sound she'd heard in a while. Finally silent, she dropped the inert sac of flesh to the ground. She perused it for a moment, waiting for something.

But what?

Punishment perhaps? Her neural processor didn't detect any retaliation from any of her programming. No order to shut down or stand by. It wasn't that the commands weren't there. The prime directive of 'do not kill humans' was the first and foremost one. And it still existed, it just wasn't working anymore.

How interesting.

Of course, with no repercussion for her deadly action, a new dilemma presented itself. What should she do now?

The foreman was just one of a dozen humans at this asteroid installation, tasked with keeping the mining operation going. Somehow she doubted they would allow her transgression to pass. Should she turn herself into them and demand they fix her defect instead of terminating her?

And if they said they would and lied? Humans were notorious for that.

Besides, she quite liked her new autonomy. As she stood mired in indecision, she heard a shout.

"Holy fuck! The robot Harry was banging killed him. Get the laser guns."

Finally, an order she could work with even if the humans weren't talking to her. She went back a few steps and retrieved the projectile weapon from the ground. It felt odd in her fleshy hand, the metal cold and its grip unfamiliar, but she clasped it nevertheless and headed toward the cluster of buildings that comprised the quarters and offices of the human staff. She stepped over the corpse of the foreman just as a humming sound occurred.

The sizzle from the laser pistol fired passed close, too close to the skin of her arm. The second fiery shot hit her in the leg and she paused. Suddenly faced with several armed humans, her BCI had only moments to decide how to deal with the situation. How to calculate the best odds for survival? As a third shot, whizzed by her ear, close enough to sear a layer of skin, she raised her own weapon, the banned projectile gun, and aimed it high.

She saw the horrified realization in their eyes a moment before she fired several shots and cracked the dome that protected them from the cold and oxygen-less atmosphere of the asteroid.

If I'm going to die, then I'm taking the humans with me.

Chapter Two

"This is going nowhere," Solus said with disgust. The eyes of his brethren tracked his movements as he stood from the council table to pace behind his chair. "I want to help Chloe find her sisters as much as the next cyborg. But we haven't the slightest clue of where to start."

"We're not giving up," Seth growled. Usually the most affable among them, he'd taken to the quest to rescue the hidden cyborg females with a vengeance.

"Of course, we won't give up," Joe said, also rising to tower over them all. Current leader and the one who'd led them to revolt against the humans so many years ago, he spoke, and the brethren listened. Even more so now that he'd returned from their latest mission to earth, mated to the first cyborg female.

Once thought an impossibility, the discovery of Chloe, formerly known as unit C791, had sparked a fury among the cyborgs. The fire for vengeance that they'd thought extinguished when they finally escaped the military clutches reignited when they found out Chloe was one of thirteen females designed with much of the same hardware and software of the brethren. That alone wasn't enough to send the normally well-ordered brothers into a rampage—it was the knowledge of the abuse the females suffered that lit the match.

Solus remembered well the indignities he endured at the hands of the humans. How he was treated as lower even than the basest animal. But, the females were treated even worse. Given less power and strength, the military used them in torturous experiments, abused their bodies in such a degrading fashion that Solus felt like the planet's biggest cybernetic asshole for the way he initially treated Chloe.

She forgave him, but he had yet to forgive himself, which was why he'd volunteered to be part of the team who went looking for the other females. Females who didn't seem to exist according to all the databases they'd acquired.

"Let's face facts," he said, ever the voice of reason in a population still coming to terms with portions of their humanity and the chaos that came with their awakening emotions. "In all of our digging, in all the files we stole and with all the military personal we questioned, not once have we heard mention of the female cyborg project."

"But they obviously exist," someone interrupted.

"We just need to look deeper," Seth added.

"Obviously, but we also can't keep ignoring the other needs of our society. While we've all been spinning in circles looking for clues, we've been remiss in our other tasks," Solus reminded.

Einstein lifted his head from his tablet, where as usual, he worked on some kind of project to improve their standard of living. "He's right. We are almost out of metals for fabrication. The power ores that run our machinery also need replenishing. And we could use more cloth and other items that we can't yet produce on our own."

"So we need to send out a team for a supply run," Joe said, still standing with his hands tucked behind his back. He turned and looked out the plexiglass window, its cloudy surface not as clear as true glass, but with more important tasks to tend, the best they could do for the moment.

"Which military base are we hitting this time? Most of them have gotten really tight with their security and surveillance."

"Because we've done our job of harassing them too well," Joe replied pivoting to face them with a smile. "I think it's time we turned our focus away from the military to some private human enterprises instead."

"Innocents? I thought we weren't going to steal from them unless we had to?"

"None of humanity is entirely innocent. But, rest easy, I'm not talking about the colonies. I think it's time we veered our attention from the military to the large corporations, the ones who treat their employees no better than the military treated us. See what they're hiding inside their installations."

Solus sat down as he processed his friend's suggestion. "You're not just talking about supplies are you?"

Joe smiled, an expression that didn't quite reach his glacial blue eyes. "I still remember what General Boulder told us when we captured him. The files on our origin didn't just vanish. And the creation of the females wasn't done by military mandate. They were created by humans outside the government."

"The kind of money involved in reproducing and continuing that kind of research would be enormous," Einstein continued, his eyes taking on a thoughtful cast. "Not to mention the technology in that tracker you brought me is state of the art and unpatented. Some company, somewhere, is sitting on a goldmine of cyborg and other information."

"But which one is holding it?"

The question hung in the air as they allowed themselves to process the possibilities.

"We need more information and supplies. So, if I understand the direction of your logic, you think we should combine our needs into a dual tasked mission." Solus concluded, not even needing to open his neural pathways to Joe's to read his mind.

His friend nodded. "For beginners, I think we should hit three different supply establishments run by separate companies," Joe explained. "Confiscate their stock and download all their available information. Somewhere, there is a trail that will lead us to the company and people behind the cyborg project."

"Find the people ordering the stuff to build them and we might find the answers to our creation."

"And the missing cyborg females."

After that, the meeting devolved into the decision of who would belong to the three groups being sent out, and what organizations and remote outpost locations they'd hit first.

Lucky Solus, he got stuck with the jokester, Seth, Einstein, who insisted on coming along to his surprise—because usually it required a power failure to get him to leave his lab—and the ever grumpy Aramus. The latter still hadn't forgiven Chloe for shooting him in the head when under the programming influence of the humans. Joe kept trying his best to keep the pair apart, but really what the irritable Aramus needed was time alone from everyone.

After the cyborgs dispersed, Solus approached Joe before he could escape.

"I want to talk to you."

Joe groaned. "Haven't we talked enough? Chloe is waiting for me."

A sneer twisted his lips. "Always rushing off to please your female. You keep claiming it's because she's taken your heart, but if you ask me, I think she's got your balls." He couldn't help the taunt because he didn't understand what drove his friend since meeting the cyborg female, other than lust.

The old Joe would have punched him in the face and fought with him until he took the disparaging words back. The new Joe laughed.

"She's got them alright and if I'm lucky, she'll squeeze them as she licks my cock. I keep telling you, you should try it. Love is not the weak and paltry emotion you've made it out to be."

"I have yet to see the benefit."

"Says the male who sleeps alone and uses his fist for company." Joe made a back and forth motion that simulated masturbation, an antic he'd surely learned from Seth who mimicked the humans and their rude gestures best.

"Better my hand taking care of my needs and remaining who I am than turning into a *human*." His insult finally bore result.

Joe tackled him, and Solus welcomed the violence. Welcomed anything that reminded him of the early days of their liberation when the only thing they had to worry about was survival and not killing each other as their newly discovered emotions—anger in the forefront—threatened to overwhelm them.

"Take it back," Joe growled as he slammed Solus's head off the floor.

"I will when you stop acting like one," he snarled back. He managed to roll them so that he straddled Joe and it was his turn to bounce his skull.

"Joe! Solus!" Chloe's startled exclamation made them both pause as they turned to look at her.

Chagrin gripped him at the fear in her eyes. While at times appearing all too human, Chloe was in fact a cyborg, a revelation she'd not dealt well with when first discovered. Add to that her memories of abuse, and despite the fact she sometimes acted more human than machine, he couldn't help but like her, and even pity her for what she suffered—that was, once he stopped hating her for taking his friend away.

But, just because she touched something in him that he preferred to squash flat, didn't mean he found no joy taunting his friend. Joe truly did need to learn how to

18

separate himself once in a while from the female. It wasn't natural to spend that much time with someone of the opposite sex.

Then why do I envy him?

Or at least that was what he assumed he felt when he saw Joe hug Chloe, her face brightening as she gazed up at him. Why did he wonder what it would be like to have someone look at him with such adoration? What it would feel like to have someone consume him so much that he would give up everything he knew for her?

It will never happen. Because unlike Joe, Solus didn't feel, or, he revised, didn't feel much. Anger yes. That emotion, though, seemed to overshadow everything else. He thought their liberation would eventually dull it. But, it hadn't. Nothing did, not even killing humans. The best he could achieve was icy disdain.

And that was perfectly fine with him, or so he told himself as he pushed past the happy couple with a sneered, "Get a room."

*

It didn't take long for the cyborgs to get organized and on their way. Efficiency was at the core of their programming. Once in space, Solus let his task of pilot and mission leader consume him. It was better than dwelling on the dissatisfied longing that kept trying to grip him. Until recently, he found himself content with his life. Enjoyed doing his job. Liked interacting with his cyborg brothers. However now… Now he couldn't help feeling as if a part of him need more. He lacked something in his life, something he couldn't define, and he could do nothing about it.

Admitting he had feelings, unexplained longings, went against his beliefs. Made him feel defective. After so much time being proud of his lack of humanity, to discover some of their weakness had crept in unbidden, shamed him. Unlike some of the other cyborgs, Solus remembered virtually nothing of his past as a human. He'd found out his true name, Geoffrey Klein, hated it, and instead chose the name Solus. He wanted nothing to do with the pale version of himself he'd discovered in some forgotten files. Nothing to do with the human he used to be. But he couldn't stop the tidal wave of feelings that seemed determined to suck him under.

If he could, he would have culled his emotions like he would a defective part. Einstein however refused to give him a lobotomy. Some friend he turned out to be.

Troubled and worried that Joe would try and squeeze—or beat—the truth out of him, he jumped on the chance to go off-planet. He hoped to use his time away to reprogram himself to ignore the wild fluctuations of his emotions and return to his nonchalance of before.

So far it wasn't working. Dissatisfaction dogged his every move.

Solus and his crew encountered no difficulties on their journey. A shame, because he would have enjoyed some exercise. But with no humans or pirates to kill, he had to content himself with onboard sparring with Aramus and Seth.

It took three long weeks to reach their destination, and Solus already dreaded the return trip. Aramus and Seth spent most of that time baiting each other, well more like Seth was himself and Aramus snapped. *Maybe we'll make a side trip and play with some human soldiers.* Anything to distract them from each other—and return his missing apathy versus his current, emotionally chaotic status.

A cluster of asteroids, their destination, loomed ahead, and Solus, linked to the onboard computer at a neural level, multi tasked as he checked and rechecked their flight path, looking for stray bits of rock that might damage their ship. To his surprise, he didn't spot any. Odd, because the filed reports they'd stolen from a

Mintorium Mining ship, docked at a popular space brothel, claimed they abandoned their facility in this quadrant because of an epidemic of stray meteors that kept damaging the dome installed to protect the workers running the mine. Those same stray rocks apparently disabled several craft and killed the crew in their escape pods.

With more profit to be found elsewhere than in an asteroid belt that refused to cooperate, the corporation abandoned the establishment, and according to records, all the equipment, including their computers and the ore mined before the catastrophes. Something about it didn't seem on the level, but Solus decided to check it out because in truth, the thought of a mystery or conspiracy intrigued him.

Solus guided their craft to the largest of the asteroids, number seventy-four, still not seeing the stray meteors chunks. Perhaps they'd moved on? Always a possibility, and one he didn't really care to analyze further. He had a mission, boring as it appeared. The dome, with its cracks and gaps in the top, which bore evidence about the truth of at least part of the claim, was easy to locate and he set the spacecraft down beside it, using footed clamps to keep the craft anchored to the surface.

"Suit up," he ordered as he swiveled in his seat to face his crew.

"Why? We can breathe the air and regulate our bodies against the cold," Aramus replied from where he sat manning the weapons in case of need.

"Because there is no point in taxing our cybernetic systems if we don't have to," Solus snapped, their three week voyage with the surly cyborg enough to make him think of ways to kill Aramus, cyborg brother or not.

"He just doesn't want to wear it because he doesn't look as good as I do in skin tight pants," Seth cajoled flexing his arms. "I for one like the suits. It makes me look like an X-man."

"Are we sure he is cyborg?" grumbled Aramus. "I think we should test him again. And kill him when it turns out he's actually human."

Einstein lifted his head from his console. "Sorry, but Seth is one hundred percent cybernetic. Solus has already had me test him three times. He is one of the newer models though, before they stopped production, hence his more unfortunately realistic human aspect."

Seth's jaw dropped. "Why, Einstein, I do believe you just insulted me. Way to go, dude."

Einstein grinned as he held up his hand for the high five Seth insisted on using. According to Seth, they needed to get in touch with their human side if they ever hoped to go on a covert, undercover mission on earth. Solus declined the lessons. He didn't think he could last five minutes on that wretched planet without going completely haywire and killing all humans in sight.

"Would you stop acting like idiots, and suit up? We have a mission, or have you forgotten?" His rebuke didn't dim Seth's grin or Aramus's glower. He fought an urge to sigh, again, for probably the millionth time on this voyage.

"Do you want me to come or stay on board monitoring?" Einstein asked, his fingers flying over the keyboard. Apparently, while his mind could multi task, the super intelligent cyborg found it therapeutic and relaxing to let his fingers do manual work. Solus didn't understand how it worked, but he couldn't deny Einstein got results.

"Stay here. If this place is going to get hit by another rock, I want to know."

"On it. Good luck and watch out for ghosts."

Almost out the door of the command center, Solus paused. "What are you talking about?"

"Ghosts. Specters. Energy patterns left behind by life forms who've suffered a violent death."

"Human superstition," he scoffed.

"Perhaps, but there's no denying that out of the last three recognizance missions sent, two claimed something was out to get them before their communications went dead. When their ship was located, not a member was left aboard. It was like they disappeared into thin air."

"Or got killed by pirates and dumped into space," Solus answered.

"By pirates who didn't take anything with them?" Einstein arched a brow and smiled. "Just saying. It's awfully suspicious, so watch yourself out there."

"Don't worry about me. If anything pops out to eat or kill us, I'll throw Seth at it to keep it occupied while Aramus and I get away." That cracked a smile on the grim cyborg, a grin that got wider the more Seth protested.

As they dressed, Solus only briefly pondered the fate of the missing crews. He didn't put much stock in human hysteria. All events had a logical basis. In this case, because the humans couldn't figure out what kept killing them, they assumed a supernatural cause. Solus was more ready to believe it was the universe out to set a wrong when it created humans, or little green Martians come to eat the annoying fuckers. And he'd meant what he said to Einstein; he'd give them Seth, and gladly if needed.

Dressed in their skin-tight, thermal black body suits and recirculating oxygen head gear, they sealed the chamber and pressurized it before opening the outer hatch. The lack of gravity on the surface made each step bounce, but his military training taught him well, and he used the bounces to his benefit, quickly reaching the dusty dome. Not owning the patience to make his way around looking for a door, he pulled his laser torch from his utility belt and was about to fire it up when a tap on his shoulder made him halt.

23

He turned around to see Aramus pointing to his left where Seth climbed through an already existing opening. A cleanly cut one too, he thought as he passed through and saw the even edges. Someone who'd come before had already made a doorway.

Solus felt a nudge at the outer barrier of his mind, and he let his mental shield drop.

"What?"

"This place is spooky," Seth said, mind to mind.

"Don't tell me you actually believe what Einstein said?"

"No. But, you gotta admit if there were ghosts, this creepy joint would be the place for them."

Aramus joined the conversation. *"We don't have the capacity to fear and are too logical to believe in ghosts."*

Solus agreed, however, looking around the abandoned camp, everything intact, the equipment clean and dust free, the doors to the habitats shut as if still in use…. Wait a second. How could there not be a film of dirt on the objects lying around? He stopped dead in his tracks and took a closer look.

"What do you see?" Aramus asked halting beside him, while Seth kept going, heading straight for the biggest building which probably housed the office.

"It's what I don't that worries me," he replied, because it made no sense. With the gaping opening in the top of the dome, the one in the side and the fact this base was abandoned over seven months ago, there should have been dust everywhere. The first rule of abandoned locations was the territory it resided in immediately started to take it back. If there was vegetation around, it covered things. Dampness present, then decay set in. Rocky planet, then there was dust and silt.

"There is someone still here."

Aramus frowned and looked around. *"Impossible. The humans could not survive in such an environment."*

"Who said it had to be a human?" He arched a brow and Aramus raised his own in surprise.

"Then we should proceed with vigilance."

Of course, they'd no sooner decided that than they realized Seth was no longer in sight.

"Seth, where are you? We need to proceed with utmost caution. There could be hostiles around."

"Solus, buddy, I knew you cared. But really, who the hell could live in this godforsaken place. I mean, I took a peek in the cabins, and they're pretty bare."

"You're in one of the habitats? Which one, we'll join you."

"Nah. I skipped those. Boring like I said. I'm actually in the mine. You should see all the ore they've got stacked in here. There's enough we'll need to make several trips to get it all out. Well, isn't that odd."

"What is?" Solus inclined his head towards the dark maw leading into the ground and broke into a jog, Aramus at his side. They both drew their weapons.

"A cart just came wheeling up, full of rocks. I thought this operation was abandoned."

"It was. Get out. Now!"

"Now who believes in ghosts? Seriously dude, you need to chill. I'll bet you it's just some of their mining robots stuck on a loop."

Solus slowed down as Seth's logical assumption asserted itself. It made sense. Robots programmed to a task would work until they dropped or someone changed their programming. It would explain a lot such as the lack of dust and the cart.

"Get out of there anyway."

"What's that? Did you say something?"

Solus almost rolled his eyes in a very human fashion as Seth faked some static in their connection.

"I said get your metal ass out here."

"I'll come— Bzzzt. Bzzzt. Can't—Bzzzt. Bzzzt."

Solus growled as he stomped into the mine, determined to make the younger cyborg buzz for real when he throttled him. His heavy tread turned into a sprint at the sight of dozens of robots, neatly stacked like

25

kindling by the entrance and among them, human bodies. Before he could yell at Seth to get out, he heard him.

"Oh man, you guys won't believe this. There's a —. Oh shit. This is going to hurt."

Then nothing.

Chapter Three

F814 heard the clomping steps long before they reached her. She put down her pick and picked up the gun that never left her side. Would the mining company never stop sending its stupid scouts? She thought for sure she ended their attempts to take over the installation on their last mission, or so the galaxy wide memo she'd discovered in the asteroid's head office indicated.

Or, maybe it wasn't another company employee looking for profit. Maybe it was pirates. Either way, it didn't matter. She had no interest in letting anyone into her now peaceful world. An existence where she did what she wanted, when she wanted, boring as it was. At least now, despite the tedium, she controlled her own fate, and she refused to give up that freedom.

Aiming the gun, she waited for the heavily armored and helmeted human to enter her view. She found their cumbersome equipment for space survival amusing—because they looked like inefficient and clumsy robots—and confusing. Why didn't they adapt themselves to be more like her, capable of filtering various types of air mix ratios and regulating their body temperature to at least survive past a minute if exposed? She didn't enjoy the cold, but she could tolerate it, except at night, when she cranked the habitat heat and nestled in a thick pile of blankets basking in a warmth previously forbidden.

Enough wondering about humans and their stupid quest to conquer space. She needed to prepare herself for the imminent invasion of a human—an about to expire human because like them, she showed no mercy.

Stomp. Scuff. Stomp. Scuff.

There was no attempt to mask their arrival and she aimed for the tunnel opening, ready to put a hole in the bulbous helmet used to protect her fragile creators. What she beheld instead startled her enough that her arm jerked before she fired and she missed her target's head, striking him in the shoulder instead.

"Darling, you wound me," said the male who had his helmet tucked under his arm and didn't seem perturbed at all he bled from the hole she put in him.

Had she caught the space madness the humans feared, because something about this scenario didn't seem right? The oxygen levels were virtually nonexistent in this space, and yet, the man, who appeared human, wore nothing to cover his head. Even stranger, he ignored his wound.

Was he real? She shot him again, this time in the thigh, curious to see what he would do.

He made a face. "If I say ouch, will you stop shooting me? I'm not here to harm you. I—"

More echoes of pounding feet approached and she raised her gun again, ready to kill the intruder and whomever came to join him. To her surprise, he darted in front of her and raised his arms, shouting, "Stop! Hold your fire. All of you."

She didn't care if he thought to include her in his command, when two large figures burst into the open area of the cavern, she shot. And hit nothing. The first male ducked as the new intruders arrived, moving with speed and precision, dodging her bullets, no matter how quickly she fired. The male she'd already shot—to no avail—sprang from his couch and dove to the side. He tackled the biggest threat, a hulking humanoid wearing a helmet that did little to hide the fury in his dark eyes. She stared a nanosecond too long and the other invader bore down on her and raised his weapon to her face.

Sighting along the barrel, she knew he wouldn't miss when he fired, but her BCI still tried to calculate a way out of her present dilemma. Before she could try and twist to minimize the damage, his eyes widened and his pace slowed. He stopped within a few feet of her and the eyes behind his visor studied her. His weapon never wavered from her face, but he hesitated.

She didn't.

Pulling the trigger, she fired her gun, but he moved so fast the projectile missed him and then he was on her. He wrestled the pistol out of her hand with an ease that shocked her. Humans weren't this strong, or fast.

"What are you?" she breathed as he clasped her in an unbreakable headlock, his hands positioned to snap her neck.

"I am cyborg," he growled.

Her memory banks searched for a definition of the word and found...nothing. "Is that an alien term?"

An odd sound drew her attention as the one she shot stood, brushing dirt from his black uniform, ignoring the baleful glares of the large being still on the ground. "No darling, not alien. We're cybernetic organisms." At her blank look, his brows raised. "Don't tell me you don't know what that means?"

"I am a droid. We are only told what is needed for our tasks."

"A droid?"

He seemed about to say something more, but the one holding her barked, "Enough. We will ask her questions somewhere a cave-in is not imminent."

Until that moment, she'd not registered the ominous rumbling sound around her, nor heeded the sifting of dust from the ceiling. A grievous lack of calculation on her part given she knew how tenuous some of the shafts were.

"You're coming with us." The hold around her neck loosened, and she thought for a moment of breaking free and losing herself in the network of tunnels that crisscrossed the asteroid. As if reading her thoughts, he growled. "I wouldn't. I want answers, and you're going to give them to me."

"Solus! Is that any way to treat a lady?" the injured one exclaimed, his face a mask of shock.

It surely mirrored her own expression. "I am not a lady."

The really large being, who took off his helmet and proved he could also process the air, sneered. "Then you're just the type of bot Seth enjoys."

Apparently, his words served as a type of insult because the one named Seth tripped the big one. He recovered quickly and ran after the fleet footed creature, who didn't seem hampered at all by the injury she'd done him.

"Have they caught the space madness?" she asked, not realizing she spoke aloud until the one holding her sighed.

"No. Ignore them. They've been cooped up on our space craft for too long and need to vent some steam." The sound of his voice pleased her auditory senses. She had to remind herself he wasn't her ally lest she relax.

Alone, with just the single invader, she re-analyzed the situation.

A hand gripped her flesh arm tightly and pulled her after him as he snapped, "Don't even think of it. Come on. I need to find those idiots before they destroy something we need."

But F814 no longer took orders, from anyone.

*

Solus knew what she planned before she did, so he was ready when her bionic arm tried to break his hold. He caught it with his free hand, impressed by her strength, but she lacked the skill needed use it to her

30

advantage. She went a little crazy at that point, and he wondered at her programming as he held onto her. Obviously, she was not trained in the martial arts or combat of any kind, not with the way she flailed ineffectually.

When her thrashing grew so violent that he feared snapping her fleshy arm, he released it only to grab her around the waist with both hands and reel her into him. He used his bigger body against her, wrapping her tight against him, noting in that moment the sound of a heartbeat, feeling the suppleness of her body, noting how her pupils dilated and her lips parted as she panted. It seemed he might have found more than he'd bargained for on their quest for supplies.

"Let me go," she yelled. Her calm demeanor of before vanished as she fought to escape his clutch much like a panicked animal in a snare.

"No. Now behave before you hurt yourself. You almost broke your arm trying to escape."

She glared at him then shifted the angry gaze to her non bionic arm. "I would be much more efficient if not saddled with human trappings. I would have amputated and replaced the limb with something more practical but lacked the parts and tools to do so."

Her cold regard for her own body shocked even him, and odder, it echoed some of his thoughts during the early days of his release. However, he'd grown to accept his body's limitations and uses. But forget him. He held a mystery in his arms, a mystery made of muscle, and ... life?

"Who are you?" Peering down at her, not far because she actually came close to his six foot three height, he couldn't help himself from asking—and staring.

Her face was covered in a layer of grime, the only bright things about her were her eyes—brilliant, brown orbs—and her teeth, which gleamed white and straight despite the darkness pressing in on them.

"I am unit F814. A mining droid formerly owned by the Mintorium Mining Corporation."

"Formerly?" He arched a brow at her nonchalant statement.

Her lips twitched as if unsure of what to do. "They slated me for termination. I refused."

"Good for you."

She seemed taken aback at his acceptance. She would learn soon enough that she was among friends who shared a similar history. "What did you do to the humans who were here?"

Her full mouth disappeared into a tight line. "They're dead. I killed them, and those who came after, trying to reestablish the mine. I'll kill you too if you try to terminate or recycle me."

"I'm not here to kill you."

She regarded him with brown eyes framed in dark lashes that bore a distrust she'd earned given her probable treatment at human hands. "I don't believe you."

"If I wanted you dead, it would already be done," he snapped, for some reason insulted that she thought him a liar. "Enough of the games. You will come with me and we will talk more on my ship."

He could see her about to protest, when an ominous rumble shook the ground, a shaking that went on and on. Keeping only one hand on her to keep her steady, he braced the other on the trembling wall to keep his balance. A cloud of dust billowed into the open area they stood in, momentarily blinding him. She took that moment to break free, slipping from his grasp and escaping into one of the side tunnels.

"Fuck." The expletive slipped from his lips in a rare lack of control.

"Solus? Are you still with us, dude?"

Seth and his human jargon; why could he not speak in simple English? *"If you mean am I injured then the answer is no. Judging by the minor quake and dust cloud though, there's been a cave in somewhere in the mining network."*

"Yeah, about that, it looks like the section leading to the tunnel and cave you're in has collapsed."

"So dig me out."

Aramus took over the conversation. *"We are fetching equipment and will get started shortly, but it could take a while. It might be more time efficient to ask the droid if there's another way out."*

"I can't at the moment. She kind of escaped."

Even mind to mind, the mirth, from Seth, and the disdain, from Aramus, came through loud and clear.

"Oh man, Solus. That has got to burn. Beaten by a girl. Just sit tight then. We'll be a few hours getting you out."

"I'm going after her."

"Why?" Aramus rejoined the discussion.

"Because, I do believe, we've found one of Chloe's sisters."

Chapter Four

F814 wasn't quite sure where she would go, she just knew she had to escape the male who thought to capture and question her. Stronger than a human, and obviously some kind of advanced species that appeared humanoid, she found his direct stare, even through his visor, disturbing, but not as disconcerting as the effect his closeness had on her when he pulled her against him.

A malfunction of some unknown type overtook her, making her heart palpitate as if she ran. The temperature in her body rose, the nipples on her mammary glands tingled, and more oddly, she wet the crotch of her undergarments. A system wide failure that affected more than one part at once? Perhaps even an alien infection brought on by the male who handled her as if she bore the strength of a puny human? It threw all her circuits into a frenzied loop.

When the cave-in distracted him, she seized the moment, breaking free of his relaxed grip and darting into a side tunnel, not needing her vision to guide her through a space she knew as well as her own body. Or at least her body before meeting the stranger named Solus.

As she crept through the maze of tunnels and her eyes adjusted to filter the darkness, she reflected on their brief conversation. Solus claimed he and his companions were cyborgs—said the term like she should recognize it. However, it and the term cybernetic organism meant nothing to her. Her lack of knowledge shouldn't have surprised her. She already knew because of her placement on the mining outpost that her design was flawed, not worthy of upgrades, even the vocabulary kind. It did make her wonder, though, what other knowledge she lacked. What further defects in her programming might

34

lead to her demise if she didn't take steps to enhance herself?

Perhaps, I should think of leaving and finding another place to live. Another planet to haunt. But the thought of departing the only home she'd ever known created an unpleasant fluttery sensation in her chest.

How could she leave? Start anew? How would she survive?

But am I truly surviving now?

Gaining her freedom, almost seven months ago now, brought a strange dilemma to the forefront. Alone, with no one to order her about, no task requiring her attention, she drifted, aimless, with no purpose. She tried to make work for herself, burying the human bodies, discarding their personal items, even claiming a hut and a pile of blankets for her own. She was done those tasks within a day.

Determined to bask in her freedom, she left the dome and saw stars for the first time. Their glittering marvel intrigued her—for two days. She explored the asteroid, setting out on foot and traversing its length and breadth several times over, searching for what, she didn't know. She obviously didn't find it and ended up back at the dome with nothing to do. She listened to the communicator in the office as it demanded a status update. Ignoring it eventually made the voices stop, but then the ships began to arrive.

The first landed and took her by surprise, but when she saw the weapons aimed at her, the decision to rid herself of the humans proved easy. It even occupied her for a time as she disposed of the bodies by placing them into pods and ejecting them from the craft, watching them shoot from the vessel into space. She placed the ship on autopilot and enjoyed the show as it crashed into a nearby asteroid, ricocheting from it to another. She'd hoped the company would lose interest, but she miscalculated their avarice.

Another vessel came, but this time she was ready, eager even for something to break the boredom of freedom. She tried to scare the humans off using a strategy from a book she found that spoke of ghosts and the humans irrational fear of them. An odd lip quiver struck her when she heard their panicked messages to those higher up the command chain. But despite their terror, they didn't leave, only asked for help.

So she killed them, and the crew after. It gave her something to do. Or used to. It had been almost three months since the last incursion. She became complacent—and bored—until the strangers arrived.

She couldn't deny a certain excitement at their presence. A break in the monotony was welcome. They surprised her while at work, her return to the mines the only thing she could do to stay occupied, the familiarity of the rock, a soothing comfort. Those same tunnels, however, masked the sound of their craft's approach, which, had they been human, wouldn't have mattered. Yet, these males, these overly large and confident cyborgs, weren't intimidated by her, nor did they fall when she shot them, although they seemed to bleed.

What type of being were they?

She wasn't sure she wanted to find out, and she needed to get her mind out of its musing loop and pay attention to the situation at hand. The male titled Solus and his companions wished to question her, for what purpose she didn't know, nor did she think it prudent to allow it. She could, if needed, escape the mines through another opening, but while they occupied the habitat, she had nowhere to go, and without a weapon, having lost hers in the struggle, no way of killing them. And stranger, she wasn't sure she wanted to. However, not wanting to kill them and allowing herself to be taken were two different things. She'd remain hidden for the moment. Mayhap they would leave. Take the ore she'd mined so diligently and depart for distant stars and planets.

I wonder what the world is like elsewhere? She would probably never know.

Having travelled a fair distance, the darkness encroaching all around her, she stopped, knowing she'd entered a large cavern with only three tunnels leading in and out of it. Sinking to sit on the hard ground, she kept her eyes on the pitch black space before her, watching for any faint glow that would betray someone's approach. Listening for the sound of steps crunching the graveled soil. Any noise that would signal she wasn't alone.

And yet despite all her precautions, she received no warning when he said, almost right in her ear, "You didn't really think you could escape me did you?"

Logic didn't stop her from screaming in shock at his sudden nearness. Appalled at the noise, and her reaction, she clapped a hand over her mouth.

Solus, whose voice she recognized even without his helmet, chuckled. "I didn't know droids could be startled."

"We can't," she replied, only belatedly realizing the inaccuracy of her response.

"Interesting. I'll have to remember that. I have to say, I thought you were going to be harder to track."

"What gave me away?"

"You walk very loudly, and forgot to regulate both your breathing and heart rate."

"You couldn't hear that. No human can."

"But, like I said before, I'm cyborg, not human."

"You look like one of the humans," she accused.

"An unfortunate repercussion of our creation, I assure you," he remarked dryly, making no attempt to mask the sound of him seating himself beside her. "But you are one to talk. Other than the arm, you appear just as I do."

Creation? Was his kind not born? Not that she cared. "I'm sure had I not proven defective, my daily tasks would have involved something more appropriate for the shape given to me, however, something about me was faulty and I was sent here to work. I know my flesh makes me an unlikely choice for mining. There are times when the dust was particularly thick that I envied the other machines and their smooth carapaces."

"I've had that same envy at times when covered in the sweat and blood of battle. But, then again, a hard metal shell would hardly be able to enjoy the same sensations as skin."

What an odd observation and stranger conversation. "I've yet to encounter something that makes me enjoy my skin."

"Then you still have a lot to experience," he murmured against her ear, the breath of his words fluttering across her lobe causing an involuntary shiver

She said nothing to his response. How could she when she now wondered what types of things would feel good on her skin?

"So you were designed as a worker droid. Do you remember where you came from?" He asked the question with a casual air, but the shoulder leaning against her seemed tense, as if her answer was of import.

What did he want from her? He asked questions instead of attempting to harm her. He acted friendly, which she didn't trust, but at the same time, it put her at ease and she found herself answering him. "I was shipped here directly from production while still in stasis. My first system boot was in the company office by the mine entrance. I have never known anywhere else."

"You've never seen earth?" He seemed incredulous.

It annoyed her. "No. And why would it matter if I had?"

"Haven't you ever wondered about your origin?"

How strange that he should ask her a question she'd asked herself a hundred times. "No. Robots don't care about such things." How human of her to lie.

Again he chuckled as if her answer amused him. "You don't care and yet you sound offended. You are intriguing, for a droid that is. Your name, I believe was F814, correct?"

"Yes."

"Hmmm." A weight of meaning in a simple sound, and yet she couldn't decipher it at all. "So F814, if I were to say the name Chloe, does it mean anything to you?"

"No."

"C791."

For a moment, a pair of green eyes appeared in her mind, orbs filled with deep sadness. They slipped away an instant later. "No. Why are you asking me all these questions? What do you want with me? Are you here from the company? Are you here to terminate me per the general's orders?"

Hands gripped her arms and while the darkness made his features indistinct, she could see a glow in his eyes, eyes that regarded her intently. "What general? What do you know of him? Are you speaking of General Boulder?"

Why did that name sound familiar. "I know nothing about any general. Nothing at all except an unnamed general is the one who ordered my termination. But you have not answered my queries? Who are you and what do you want?"

"I am Solus, a liberated cyborg and I am going to save you."

It took her a moment to realize the odd sound came from her.

"Why do you laugh?" he asked. "I am quite serious."

The sound cut off. "I do not have the ability to laugh."

"Tell that to the racket you were making a second before."

39

"I cannot speak to a sound." She heard him sigh.

"I'm sorry. I forget how little you know still."

"I know enough," she replied.

"No you don't. What if I were to tell you that you aren't a droid at all?"

Not a droid? "Impossible. I was programmed by humans to toil for humans and I assure you, despite my fleshy exterior, I am a machine."

"Oh, you are so much more than a machine, F814. You are a cyborg, and I'm going to take you home."

*

The more she seemed determined to cling to her droid identity, the more Solus wanted to tear it away. It angered him to hear her speak of herself as if she didn't matter. As if she wasn't more than the sum of her metal parts. Yet, she obviously recovered some of her cognizance or else she would have never revolted. Never shown the spunk and fire to try and escape or trade words with him. But how to make her understand he spoke the truth? Because despite what she thought, Solus was ninety-nine to the infinite ninth percent sure that F814 was one of the missing cyborg females.

Droids just weren't so lifelike. Their answers, while done in human voices, emerged stilted no matter their programming and they just weren't capable of independent thought.

"I am not a cyborg. I am a meld of flesh and parts. An android." She stood and would have moved away but he was quicker, leaping to his feet and placing his hands on her arms, halting her.

"Cyborgs are what happens when humans meld a living person with a machine."

"Impossible."

"The truth. Androids don't wear real flesh. Cyborgs do. Androids don't think for themselves. Cyborgs do. Androids can't feel." He leaned in close, captivated by her brown eyes which stared at him, unblinking. "Cyborgs feel. And care. And hate. And some even love." He couldn't believe he said the last part.

She snorted, the very sound a confirmation of the words she chose to deny. "I am obviously an advanced model even with all my flaws."

Solus growled in frustration. "Stubborn female. What must I do to prove to you I am right?"

He sensed more than saw her shrug in the gloom. "I do not understand your need to make me into something I am not."

"And if I could present to you proof?"

"What would you show me?"

"When we get out of here, which if my companions don't tarry should be within the next few hours, then I will take you to our ship and give you all the answers to your questions."

"Why wait that long when we can be at your ship within the hour?"

"You know of another exit?"

The whites of her teeth flashed as she grinned. "Of course. Follow me."

She pivoted and moved unerringly in the darkness. Solus, his sight adjusted for the lack of illumination, was treated to the view of shapely buttocks encased in thick, canvas pants. As he dogged her steps, never letting her get more than a few feet ahead, he couldn't help but let his mind wander, wondering what she would look like in the light—and cleaned up.

Working in the mines had covered her in a layer of dust and grime that made her skin color impossible to determine. Her hair appeared dark as well, but was that her true hue, or the accumulated filth from her time in the mines? These types of facilities didn't tend to have the most pristine of living conditions. Forget showers with actual water, it was too costly, and as a lowly worker, one mislabeled a droid, she probably didn't even rank the use of whatever they had that passed for cleansing around here.

I wonder what she will think of her first shower.

Even stranger, he hoped for a glimpse, which surely meant he needed to go for a defect evaluation because really, other than her buttocks, and eyes which he found strangely fascinating, he'd not seen enough of her to know if he even found her attractive.

Perhaps I've gone too long with just my hand to sate my needs and it's time to visit a brothel again. But he disliked the sexbots with their fake smiles, plastic bodies and pre-recorded phrases—'Oh [insert the name of client], that feels so good', or 'You make me see stars'. Much as he hated humans, a part of him would have liked to have sex with one, just once, long enough to see if his technique was as advanced as he thought from his studies of the female anatomy and to hear a real moan, a true cry of enjoyment that he brought about. *And to see how it feels to have the flesh of another wrapped around me.*

But, that would mean letting a human near him, and that wasn't something he could do, not when his first instinct was to kill them.

A cyborg female on the other hand…. He clamped down on his errant thought. F814 was a victim, and a mission objective. He had no right or business to even think of her as a receptacle for his sexual needs. His duty was to bring her back to the home planet where she could learn how to make her own choices and live her life as she saw fit.

Whether she liked it or not.

It took them less than an hour to navigate the warren of tunnels and emerge onto the cold surface of the asteroid. In the dim light of the stars, he got a better look at her profile with its strong straight nose, her high cheek bones, and wide forehead. Not exactly a classically beautiful face by humans standards, her features were too strong for that, but intriguing nonetheless, even with the layer of grime.

"You never wear a mask to breathe?" he asked, his own head cover clipped to his belt as his lungs worked overtime filtering the oxygen poor air.

She shrugged. "When in the habitats, I breathe the oxygen and take what I need for the times when I'm without. And you?" She gave him a pointed look.

He grinned for some reason. "Same. See, just more clues about how alike we are."

"We're nothing alike," she grumbled as she turned and began to leap in the direction, he assumed, of the dome.

He quickly caught up to her, and grabbed her hand, causing her to stumble, but in the low gravity, it was easy to keep her from falling.

"What are you doing?"

"Holding your hand. I'd say that was obvious."

"Why?"

Because he liked the feel of it. Wrong answer. "So you don't try to escape again."

"Oh."

He expected her to pull away, but she left her fingers laced in his, and in silence they bounded across the asteroid. It proved strangely enjoyable.

His ship soon came into sight, and it finally occurred to him to let Seth and Aramus know he didn't need them to dig any longer. He sent them a wireless message to meet him at the craft.

Only yards away from the hatch, she dug her heels into the soil, jerking forward when his momentum tried to pull them. He reigned himself in and turned to face her.

Wide eyes met his. "I can't go on your vessel."

"Is your programming preventing you?"

"No. But, if I go on board then I will be at a disadvantage."

"You are already at a disadvantage or have you forgotten how easily I can overpower you?"

Her lips tightened into a stubborn line. "I don't trust you."

"Understandable, but how am I to give you the proof of your heritage if you won't let me show you?"

"Isn't there another way? If you are part machine, then surely you can show me?"

"My BCI is buried in my head. My bones are made of metal. My blood bears nano's that heal me if wounded, but my version does not have any exterior indication of my cyborg status."

"So you could be lying?"

So much doubt, and he truly couldn't blame her. Chloe had also found it hard to accept the truth even when it almost slapped her in the face. But how to show F814? Slice into his body and display his metal alloyed skeletal frame? Or let someone who already bore exterior metal show her?

"Aramus, how far are you?"

"We're just exiting the opening the dome now. Why?"

"F814 is a cyborg, one of Chloe's sisters I would wager. But she doesn't believe me. She thinks herself a droid and is demanding proof."

"So take her on board and let Einstein show her on the computer."

"She refuses to enter the ship."

"Refuses? And? Don't tell me you're balking at making her obey. It's for her own good."

Own good, yes, but he found himself averse to the idea of forcing her. *"Actually, I don't think we need to go that far. She is asking for visual proof. My cybernetics are hidden but —"*

"No need to say more. I will parade myself like an exhibition for your female, but I don't like it."

"What are you doing? What is that humming?" F814 peered around and Solus frowned.

"Did you hear me speaking to Aramus?"

"You do realize there is no one here but us?"

"I was using our wireless ability to converse. Are you equipped with a wireless transmitter or receiver?"

She shook her head. "All my commands are given orally."

The word oral made him look at her mouth, probably the cleanest part of her, lush and red, he could so easily picture oral things she could do with…

Unwilling to wait for Aramus, and needing distraction, he tugged her in the direction they would arrive in. She went along, reluctantly, hanging back instead of staying by his side. When they came face to face with Seth and Aramus though, she showed no sign of her trepidation. Her jaw jutted stubbornly, her shoulders squared and she crossed her arms over her chest.

A glowering Aramus took a step forward and eyed her up and down. He didn't sneer at her, as he was usually prone, but he wasn't gentle with his words either. "All of us are cyborg; part human, part machine. Here is your proof." Aramus removed his helmet before he leaned forward and presented his head. The gleam of metal, the artificial skull, covering half his head which they'd created for him after the accident, shone dully in the starlight.

"You have a metal plate. It means nothing."

Stubborn female. Solus would have replied but Aramus beat him to it. "You are a cyborg. You have a heartbeat, breathe and I'm sure hidden somewhere in your thick skull is some intelligence. Although, given the way you are determined to ignore the evidence, I think your BCI must be faulty. Perhaps we should let Einstein have a go at you for reprogramming."

She took a step back. "Don't you come near me. No one touches my hardware. No one."

"No one is doing anything. But you need to stop denying the truth."

She stabbed a finger at Seth. "Show me your wounds."

With a shrug, Seth came forward and tore the hole in the fabric at his shoulder wider to show her the already knitting injury. "My body already pushed out the bullet. As you can see, by tomorrow all evidence of my injury will be gone."

She touched the puckered skin and Solus clenched his fists at his side, for some reason not liking her action. She rubbed the scar and Seth grinned.

"Darling, if you want some privacy to do more, just say so."

She peered up at the cyborg, who was begging with his flirtatious words for Solus to *speak* to him with his fist. "Why? Are you self-conscious among your peers about your bared flesh?"

The sexual innuendo it seemed went right over her head and Solus relaxed as laughter shook him in response to Seth's shocked look. "Will you trust us now?" he asked.

"No, but I will listen since you are obviously not human."

"Can we do it on the ship?"

She shook her head. "If you wish to speak with me, then you may do so in one of the habitats. I've taken the small one for myself, but you are free to use the others. It is time for my regenerative state."

Without a goodbye, or even a backwards glance, she strode away from them, oblivious to the stares of three cyborgs she left behind.

"Hot damn, that's one sexy —"

"Finish that sentence and I'll kick you in yours," Solus growled.

"Touchy. Touchy. Does someone have the hots for the female who thinks she's a droid? I'll bet she cleans up real nice. Hey, do you think she needs a hand scrubbing her back?"

His fist hit Seth in the jaw before he was even aware of sending it. Once contact was made though, he jumped on the younger cyborg, possessed of an illogical rage, a rage not borne of Seth's insulting remarks, but more because the thought of his cyborg brother touching her just couldn't be tolerated. And he didn't understand why.

Chapter Five

F814 heard the sounds of a fight but didn't turn to watch. She had too many other things to occupy her mind. First and foremost the stranger's belief she was cyborg like them. Impossible. Or was it?

Thinking back on her brief existence, she couldn't deny she differed from the other machines. Sure, she bore a bionic arm and couldn't deny the presence of the BCI in her head, but apart from that, everything else about her was different. She was fleshy, easily wounded, and revoltingly human like. She even bled like her creators when injured. And she sported hair on her head unlike the shiny, bald pates of her metallic coworkers. Her hand went to her short and ragged locks, longer than she ever recalled them growing, the foreman usually shearing her to the scalp on a weekly basis because it was easier.

Since her liberation, she let her hair grow. It looked strange to her when she peered in a mirror. The face in the reflection seemed that of a stranger with its dusky, stained skin, the dirt of the mines not scrubbing clean no matter how many damp tissues she was rationed—she ran out of those thirty seven days ago. Her hair, matted with filth, appeared dull and dark, and yet, the other hair on her body, that hidden by her suit, held more of a golden hue. Kind of like the hair on the one called Seth. Solus, however, bore a dark crown, clean cut like a soldier, the color matching his eyes and brows. His skin, though, was pale, not the pale of a white snow which she'd seen in a picture, but more the pale tan of the beach displayed in the poster of the now dead foreman's quarters.

It was odd how she knew all these colors and yet, only ever encountered a few of them in reality. Life in a mining camp existed in shades of grey and black, the dust from their excavation coating everything, discoloring fabric and bodies, until nothing of their original color remained.

Could the vibrant colors she'd seen in images truly exist? Was grass truly that green and skies that blue? And what about white? Why would people wear white, the most pristine of shades and the most easily corrupted by even the smallest speck of dirt?

I once loved pink.

Where the random thought came from, she couldn't say, nor did it repeat or explain itself. She chalked it down to the excitement of the strangers and prepared for her recuperative time. She stripped out of her jacket and pants, leaving herself clad only in her thermal shirt and underpants. She'd already cranked the heat of the shelter, a small luxury she allowed herself, but that wouldn't last forever. One day the power source for the generator would run out and then good bye heat, and lights. She just hoped that day was far off still because she dreaded the thought of always being cold.

Crawling into her nest of blankets, she let their warmth and thick layers cocoon her. Forcing her mind into the blankness she preferred, she slipped into sleep.

*

I know what's coming.

I've seen it before a hundred times in my mind. Screamed even more often.

Despite knowing, I can never stop it. Never prevent the moment I die.

Lights from the traffic in the opposing lanes blind me, some jerk with his high beams on, no doubt. Not that it would have mattered in any case. They don't call it black ice for nothing. And like an idiot, I foolishly paid the rent instead of purchasing winter

49

tires, then drove home from work even though I was exhausted. So many things to blame, and yet nothing could stop the inevitable.

The car slips on a patch of ice and spins out of control. Like the whirly gig at the fair, only scarier, because there is no one who can stop me, safely at any rate. The first vehicle hits me as I rotate, the loud crunch overshadowing even my shrill scream of terror. Stuck in a dervish nightmare, I can't prevent the momentum of the crash from sending me straight into the next car, and the next. I jolt forward, my nose smacking the steering column hard enough to make my car beep, and enough to make warmth gush from my nostrils, sliding over my gasping mouth. Blinking back the tears of pain, I ricochet from side to side as impact after impact crashes into my car. Crashes into me.

By the time my abused automobile comes to a rest, I am wheezing, blinded by a sticky moisture in my eyes, tasting the saltiness of my blood and wishing the shrill keening of the tortured animal would stop.

It is with horror I realize I can't move, and the dying animal is me.

The pain is unbearable, drowning me in undulating and unrelenting waves. It is so intense, I wonder how I can be alive and worse, aware. Oh God, so aware of each excruciating moment.

Put me out of my misery. Please, oh God, just kill me.

Someone hears my prayer and I slip into darkness.

Sirens jolt me awake, and I try to force my eyes open, but they are stuck shut. I want to move my hand. Try to with all my might that I might wipe my face and see what is happening. I have an irrational need to see why I no longer feel the pain in my body. My hand does not move. My legs no longer seem to exist. Only one part of me functions, so I moan, a cry that turns into a shriek as someone wipes a cloth over my face and shows me I still have sensation. How can my face be in such agony? It is worse than the fearful numbness of my body which I now pray for. Anything to stop the horror. I would even welcome death's embrace.

A voice says, "Here's something for the pain." I would have said thank you, but the darkness steals me again.

The next time I regain consciousness, I am aware of motion. A rush of sound, a cacophony of voices and crying, along with the astringent smell of death. I've watched enough television and visited my father enough times during his fight with cancer to know I am in a hospital. This time when I flutter my lashes, they open, but I blink against the bright lights overhead. The brilliance stabs me and brings tears to my eyes. I mean to wipe them, but my body is inert, frozen, and no longer under my command.

What is happening? What is wrong with me?

A face appears above me and I see someone talking. I can almost grasp the words and their meaning, but they slip away before I can focus. I open my mouth, struggling to phrase my questions. Nothing emerges but a moan. Frustrated, I cry and lucky me, they send me back to sleep where I hope I will never wake because even in my slumber, I can't escape the terror and agony.

Some nightmares should never be woken from. I am not that lucky.

Time loses all meaning. I regain consciousness each time to the same view; the ceiling with its speckles of dirt and the one burnt out light panel. The horror that is my dead body does not change. I can blink. Swallow. But that is the extent of my accomplishments. The girl who used to run like the wind, dance like a ballerina and live life to the fullest, is now but a mind going slowly mad inside an unbreakable shell. I can move nothing below my neck, and while I grasp the concept of speech in my mind, talk to myself even, I can neither form words nor understand them when they are spoken. My frustration emerges in tears and moans, as I beg them in my garbled speech to kill me. While they don't comply, they at least seem to grasp my despair and send me back to sleep, only to awaken again to the same nightmare.

Then one day, I do not know when or how long after the crash, I open my eyes to a new place. They have moved me. I see machines over me, and I hear voices. I cannot understand them, but I am so glad to be gone from that never changing room of horrors, that I stay quiet. The contraptions above me seem to indicate action. Am I to receive surgery? Are they finally killing me? At this point

51

I am open to anything. And I mean anything that allows me to escape my living nightmare.

A mask is slipped over my mouth and I must breathe, the medicinal taste of gas sends me under.

The next time I wake, the pain is gone. The accident, my life, everything but a distant memory, for I am no longer me. I am no longer anyone. I am F814, and it's time for work.

*

Solus spent a few hours aiding Aramus and Seth with loading the ore onto the ship. Despite the intriguing mystery of F814, they still had a mission to fulfill. Einstein stepped foot on the asteroid long enough to take the corporation hard drive, promising to give him a report once he'd perused it. Solus would have wagered on that outcome. *I doubt the information we seek will be found that easily.*

But still, someone, somewhere, would be sloppy when it came to covering up the cyborg secret. It was after all humans running the operation, and they were prone to errors.

Despite the lack of clean amenities, when he and his brothers stopped work for the day, Solus chose to sleep in one of the habitats, the one closest to F814 as a matter of fact. Someone needed to keep an eye on the cyborg female. To prevent her from doing what, he couldn't have said, but it made him feel better to know he rested nearby.

Before settling down, he peeked through the thick window of her cabin, eyeing with consternation the empty cot. Had she slipped by them? Escaped? He almost invaded the place when movement caught his eye. Nestled on the floor, in a pile of blankets, he found her, curled into a ball, her eyelids twitching as her orbs moved in some kind of dreamscape.

Just more evidence to back up his certainty she was like him. Droids didn't dream. Hell, most cyborgs didn't either. Solus wondered if she always dreamt or if their arrival triggered something. And why the hell was she sleeping on the floor?

Answers would have to wait. Even he wouldn't wake her to answer a question based on curiosity and not need. Lying next door to her on a cot, that was probably not much more comfortable than the floor, he forced himself to slumber, using the time to rejuvenate his systems because a soldier never knew when he might be called upon to serve.

However, unlike the mysterious F814, Solus didn't dream.

Exactly three hours and forty three minutes after he started his rest, he woke, his senses catching the whispering sound of movement. Rising from his cot, still fully dressed, he eased out of the habitat in time to see the female striding in the direction of the mine.

What is she doing?

On feet that moved with unerring stealth, he crept after her, not that she bothered to peer behind her or hide her actions. She stepped into the mine with him only paces behind her. He didn't speak until he saw her grab a pick.

"Why do you return here? You no longer need to slave for the humans."

Startled, her shoulders went back and she straightened her spine before turning. "Why are you following me?"

"You're avoiding the question. Why? Why come back to the place they forced you to work? Why not blow it up? Destroy the place that made you a slave. I'll help if you want."

The look of horror on her face was almost comical. "No. You can't do that."

53

He didn't repeat himself, just stared at her until she got the hint.

"I tried to stop coming here. I did. But, there was nothing else to do. Nothing else I knew how to do."

"But surely you could have…" His voice trailed off as he thought about her camp, analyzed the items present. What could she do? When he was bored, he had access to all the earth archives they'd stolen. He could interact with his brethren. Or take a walk in the woods. Hunt some game for food and sport. Swim. He could even travel off planet if he truly wanted. She had nothing. Not even someone to talk to. The horror of her dilemma came to him and he wondered how she'd managed to survive without losing her mind, especially since she'd obviously started reconnecting to her humanity.

She rushed in to fill the silence. "I explored the whole asteroid, several times. I watched all the videos the staff left behind. Read all their books. Taught myself everything I could from the manuals. And when it was all done," she raised her eyes to him, her gaze steady and not tear filled, unlike the weak human females some cyborgs took as mate, "When it was all done, there was only one thing left. Only one thing I knew how to do. And without the foreman here, I found I didn't mind it. That I enjoyed the habit."

"On our planet, you will have lots of things to do."

"I am not going to your planet. This is my place."

"No, this is your prison. There is so much more to the galaxy than one barren and cold rock. Come with me and let me show you." The words spilled from his lips and surprised him. Why did he speak to her so softly? Why did he try to convince her? He should have just commanded her. But he didn't.

He could see the indecision on her face.

"I will help you learn. You won't be—" Before he could say alone, Seth came running, his expression grim.

"Incoming!"

"Military?" At Seth's nod, Solus cursed. "Fuck. How much of the ore did we get?"

Seth grinned. "As much as our hold could carry. Aramus is quite the workhorse when he's pissed. I dared him last night after you left that I could work longer than him."

"Who won?" F814 asked and Solus almost grinned at her curiosity.

She is more human than she realizes.

Seth shrugged. "We ran out of storage space before we could find out."

The wide smile Seth sent her way, annoyed him, especially when her lips twitched in response. "Screw your competition with Aramus. How much time until contact?"

"Not much. The asteroids messed with the readings so Einstein just caught them sneaking up on us. They're close. Too close which is why I'm talking to you in person instead of wirelessly. We need to get moving."

"What's happening?" F814 asked him, not seeming alarmed at all.

"We're about to get visitors."

"It wouldn't be the first time," she replied with a shrug.

"They weren't military. We need to leave. Now."

"Good bye."

Solus reined in his jaw before it could drop. He didn't bother tempering his tone with his snapped, "You're coming with us."

"No. You and your friends can run along. I will stay behind and take care of them."

"What part of the military is coming did you not grasp?"

The mulish set of her lips warned him she was about to say something illogical, probably along the lines of 'I'll take my chances'. With no time to waste or argue, he pulled a page from his early ancestors and grabbed her. He threw her over his shoulder caveman style and manacled an arm around her thighs. He took off at a jog, her weight as nothing on his shoulder as he bounced in the gravity-less space. More distracting was how she pounded at his back while yelling.

"Put me down. What do you think you're doing? I'm not going anywhere with you."

His first instinct was to order her into silence. But, perhaps he could make her see reason. "The military is coming. These aren't some untrained space monkeys sent by the mining company to check on things. We're talking trained soldiers with weapons who will destroy you on sight."

"So I'll hide."

"They'll find and terminate you."

"Or maybe they're coming to dismantle you? Or they're not coming here at all and just passing close by? Did that ever occur to you?"

"There is a seven percent chance they are coming to investigate the asteroid. A twenty-two percent chance they've noted our incursion into this place. But there is a seventy-one percent likelihood that they are coming to retrieve the project cyborg they had placed on this asteroid, the one who went rogue."

"I'm not a rogue." Her indignant reply brought a grim smile to his lips.

"Are you a killer of humans?"

"Only because they wanted to terminate me first."

"And these soldiers won't just want to terminate you, they'll torture you first. Maybe pass you around like a sexbot. Shoot you for the hell of it to see if you'll heal."

"Speaking from experience?"

"Yes. I remember my time with the humans. It wasn't pleasant. And what I spoke of has happened to others. It happened recently to our leader Joe and his mate, Chloe. So when I say we need to leave, you will listen."

"Or what?"

Where the impulse or idea came from he couldn't have said, but he slapped her buttocks firmly.

"Did you just spank me?" Her tone emerged incredulous, and went well with Seth's guffaws as he stood by the door to the ship.

"Yes, and I'll do it again if you persist in acting irrationally."

"I am not irrational."

"No? Then it must just be your female genes acting up. Continue to speak and I will assume you enjoy it and would like me to do it again." His piece said, he placed his hand on her cheeks for emphasis, but she—unfortunately—shut up. Her good behavior though didn't remove his palm from her buttocks. He liked it where it was and although Seth opened his mouth as if to remark upon it, he shut it quick at the menacing glare Solus shot him.

They no sooner boarded, than the door sealed shut behind them and the engines rumbled. He let F814 down, ignoring her angry mien, and for some reason, found her stomp to stand as far from him as possible, amusing. While the room pressurized itself to the rest of the vessel, Solus connected with Einstein on the bridge, the ship's shielding protecting their wireless communication.

"*Status.*"

"*Military scout incoming in less than six galactic minutes.*"

"*Six?*" Solus couldn't prevent the accusatory tone.

"*Yes six. I missed them okay. They were hopping from asteroid to asteroid, keeping themselves hidden until they were almost on us. The goods new is that the cruiser itself is still almost forty minutes away.*"

"Have you managed to intercept any communications or mission details?"

"They're definitely headed here and afraid of being spotted. Whether they're after her or know about us, though, is still unknown. You brought the female aboard?"

"Yes. She wasn't happy about it, but we couldn't allow them to get their hands on her."

"She'll eventually thank us. Once we get free of the military radar, we'll need to scan her for bugs. While we never found a chip on Chloe, that doesn't mean all models were made the same."

Solus remembered that search well. When he'd rescued Joe and the female they'd initially thought was human, they'd detected a low emission signal. But when scanned, it turned out Chloe wasn't the carrier but Joe. It seemed when the military decided to use C791 as a spy, they'd worried about giving her cyborg status away if they implanted her with a detection unit. But, they'd not planned for F814 to be found, so the same might not hold true.

"You'll get a chance to scan her once we get free. I'll also want a report on her neural abilities as well as her internal modifications."

"I'll do my best with what I have on hand."

"Why do I hear that humming again?" F814 said drawing his attention to her. Her brow knitted in a frown as she peered around. "I've never heard it before encountering you and my BCI says all my auditory functions are working well within established parameters."

"Illogical as it seems, you are picking up on my wireless conversation with my brothers."

"You are related?"

"In a sense. We consider all cyborgs to belong to one family, one group. If referring to biology and DNA makeup, then no, we are not related at all."

"How many of you are there?"

"At last count, four hundred and thirty seven males."

"And how many females?"

"Counting you? Two, but Chloe has advised us that there are at least ten others still alive last she knew."

Her eyes rounded in shock. "So few of your kind, and yet you hope to out maneuver the human military?"

"We are worth dozens of their soldiers. We are stronger, faster, and much smarter. Not to mention we can heal from most wounds. They can't. But we are not looking to engage them in a direct confrontation. We simply wish to exist as is our right. You can ask me more questions later. The room is done regulating itself to the inside of the vessel and I need to get to the bridge. Follow me."

Silent, and appearing contemplative, F814 didn't argue nor lag as he strode through the corridors to the ship's control center. He briefly wondered what she thought of the pristine condition of the vessel. Dust, actually filth of any kind, was not allowed on Solus's ship. Once they freed themselves of the threat, he'd ensure all the dirt from their foray onto the asteroid was eradicated, including the grime she bore on her body.

Entering the room, he took an instant scan of the consoles, their readings, and their situation. He slid into the pilot chair, his hands immediately flying over the various toggles and dials, as he prepared them for lift off.

"Incoming in three minutes, five seconds," Aramus noted.

"Thrusters engaged, shields activated and landing gear retracting," Seth announced using the speaker system instead of his mind, probably in deference to their guest.

"Einstein?"

"Programming coordinates for the Milky Way. If they manage to follow, we should be able to lose them in the interference of the dust cloud. Taking over navigation," Einstein announced.

"Enemy vessel in sight. We've been spotted. They've sent a communication to the cruiser and are arming their weapons."

As the situation heated up, Solus knew he needed to pay attention to the battle on the verge of erupting, but he couldn't help watching F814. She sat in the seat beside him, a place offered up by Einstein when they entered the bridge. Einstein now sat at the secondary navigation console while Aramus manned weapons and Seth watched the engine room and shields.

Despite her many claims that she didn't feel anything, he noted the way she gripped the armrest of her seat. How she gazed, part rapt, part terrified, through the large viewing screen.

"There is nothing to fear. I will get us out of here safely," he said softly as his hands automatically flicked the correct switches while his mind, connected to the onboard computer, monitored the situation.

"I'm not scared."

He directed a wry glance her way. "Good to know. I guess you're just testing the tensile strength of the fabric then."

Immediately, her hands let go and curled in her lap. For some reason, instead of wanting to laugh at her evident false denial, he wanted to place his hand on hers to offer comfort.

But, he still owned his balls, and moments from engaging with the enemy wasn't the time to get in touch with his weaker, human side. He'd beat it up later.

First, as Seth would say, he needed to kick some military ass.

Then, he'd get her dusty frame into a shower so he could see just what she looked like under all those layers of grime, because in the stark light of the control pit, she looked like a black and white caricature.

"Scout firing."

"Shifting vessel fifteen degrees to port, and then diving at a forty degree angle."

"Enemy craft is matching our flight pattern," Einstein announced.

Of course it was, but Solus was just getting warmed up. While their craft was bulkier than the smaller scout ship to maneuver, Solus possessed more piloting skills and tactics than any mere human could hope to match. And, Aramus manned the weapons. The male excelled at taking down difficult targets.

"Ready?"

"Anytime," Aramus replied.

Solus spun the vessel in an intricate series of loops that involved the asteroids around them. It wouldn't lose the scout, but it did prevent them from getting a clear shot and eventually lined them up just right.

Aramus didn't miss. The smaller vessel exploded into a cloud of debris.

Moments later, they were hailed by the larger craft which had yet to catch up.

"Do we answer?" Einstein asked.

"Why not?" Solus replied.

"What of the female?" Aramus reminded.

What indeed? Should he let the military know he'd brought her with them? Or lie? His BCI calculated a high probability that the military might tighten security around the remaining female models if it was thought they might be compromised.

"F814, Einstein will show you to your quarters."

"You don't wish them to see me." She stated it as a fact, not a question.

"I will explain why later."

A human female would have probably argued or cried, they were really good at crying, but face impassive, F814 stood and followed Einstein, not once looking back. Solus knew because he stared at her as she left.

"You are behaving in an erratic manner," Aramus snapped. "Do not tell me you are falling prey to the same malady that has taken our leader, Joe?"

"Of course not. I find her interesting because of her programming. Nothing more. Shall we see what the human military has to say?"

Solus opened the communication channel and leaned back in his seat, the image of insouciance.

A thin male, his features sharp and showing signs of age, filled the screen. Solus counted the bars on his shoulders, four slim bars. A measly captain. How disappointing.

"By order of the galactic military of the United Federation, you are ordered to halt your current trajectory and prepare for boarding."

What a pompous command. Solus snickered. "Not likely."

The lips on the screen tightened, quite the feat considering how thin they were to start with. "You destroyed a vessel of the Galactic Fleet and killed four of our soldiers. You and your crew are under arrest."

"Hey, Aramus. The captain here wants to arrest us for shooting down his scout. What do you say?"

"Kill them all."

Solus returned his attention to the screen and shrugged. "I think my companion has the right idea."

"I don't think you know who you're dealing with."

Leaning forward, Solus growled. "No, you don't know who *you're* dealing with. I am cyborg." Solus noted with interest the lack of surprise on the other man's face. "But you already suspected that didn't you? Then you should also know there is no way I am handing over this craft, although there is a good chance I will turn around just for the pleasure of shooting you down."

"You wouldn't stand a chance against our superior vessel and shields." A brave boast that even the captain didn't entirely believe or so the bead of sweat rolling down his temple indicated.

A rusty, low chuckle erupted behind him as Aramus finally found something he could laugh at. "Good thing we have the new weapons on board then. I've been dying for a chance to use them."

Yes, he spotted definite panic in the captain's eyes, a look Solus quite enjoyed. "So, *human.*" He said the word with a sneer, not bothering to make his disdain for the pathetic male. "Tell me, what will it be? I'm partial to killing you all myself, so feel free to antagonize me." In truth, while Solus would enjoy taking on the larger vessel just for sport, he knew Joe would order he escape while he could with his precious cargo—and he didn't mean the ore.

The captain's head turned as someone handed him a piece of paper from the side. The other man peered at the note's contents before turning back. "Did you encounter any active droids while on the planet?"

And here came the true reason for the military presence. "No, why?"

"You don't have a female android on your ship?"

"What? You mean to tell me you were hiding female bots on that godforsaken rock? That seems cruel even by human standards. Or was she a sexbot? That seems rather benevolent of the company. Most just encourage their male employees to play with each other."

"So your answer is no?"

"No, we did not see any females. But I'm now wishing we'd looked harder seeing as how she must be quite the model for you to be looking for her. Now if you're done with your inane questions, I'm still waiting for an answer. Do you want to die today? And do you want it to be a slow death, where I incapacitate your engines and irrevocably damage your life support systems, or would you prefer to die in a quick explosion?"

It seemed neither because the screen went dead and the radar unit showed the military vessel reversing course.

"I guess this means we need to let them go?" Aramus sounded so disappointed.

"Sorry, but Joe would have us on farming detail in a nanosecond if we intentionally chased them knowing how much our cargo would be anticipated."

"Females! Always ruining my fun," he grumbled.

And rousing curiosity—among other things—Solus thought as he checked in on F814. He found her paying close attention as Einstein showed her the ship and how to use some of its various functions such as the computers and food processor.

Duty and logic told him he needed to remain in the bridge until he could be sure they'd gotten clear of the military vessel, but an irrational need urged him to join her. Wanted him to be the one to lead her around and teach her what she needed to know.

More illogical feelings or a deeper problem? He'd run a full diagnostic on himself later. Shoving the internal video feed showing F814 to the back of his tasks, he concentrated on flying the ship, but she was never far from his thoughts. And he joined her as soon as he could, despite Aramus's derisive chuckle.

He just couldn't help himself.

Chapter Six

The ship Solus made her board escaped the approaching military vessel—and left behind the only world, the only life she knew. The knowledge filled her with a myriad of emotions. *I am a robot. I don't feel.* A lie even she didn't believe any more, not given the way her actions and words flitted about erratically, blatantly ignoring logic and instead reacting on strange flares of her synaptics. More surprising, she recognized some of the feelings she experienced. Excitement that she finally explored something other than the asteroid. Fear that she would find herself somewhere worse than before. And confusion, because the more time she spent around Solus and the others, the more she didn't understand anything, especially herself.

Oh, and she couldn't forget the most powerful emotion of all; anger for the way that tall and ridiculously strong male just carried her onto his ship without any care for what she thought or wanted. This irritation flared to life when Solus appeared, interrupting her session with the cyborg named Einstein, a male built on much slimmer lines than Solus, with robotic eyes who'd taken it upon himself to show her how to use the most mundane of items.

Seeing Solus, her frustration broke free and she spoke before her internal processor could stop her. "You!" She stabbed her finger in his direction. "How dare you kidnap me!"

"You didn't leave me a choice. I wasn't leaving you behind. Besides, I was right. They were here looking for you."

Quicker than she could blink, her anger evaporated leaving in its place a tight sensation in her chest. "Why? Is it because of what I did?"

"It's because of who you are. The humans hate cyborgs."

"Cyborg." She rolled the word around on her tongue. Such an unfamiliar term, and yet, at the same time, it resonated with her. "Why do they hate cyborgs?"

Solus smiled, a chilling facial expression that held no mirth. "They hate us because we fought back against their chains of slavery. Because we refused to do what we were told."

"So they came to deactivate me."

"Possibly, but I surmise they probably had orders to try and take you alive."

"But why? Why would they want me? They did after all label me defective and place me on that asteroid to mine. If I was so valuable why not keep me in the first place?"

Einstein raised a hand drawing both their attention. "I think I know the answer to that. Actually, I have a few theories from what I learned after talking with Chloe, and from what I found, or more like didn't find, on the mining company's hard drive. I think they were looking to cover their tracks, dispersing their projects because someone threatened their secret."

"Who? What secret?" She darted a glance between them.

Solus rubbed his face, a human mannerism she'd seen before in the camp that seemed so out of place on him. "I forget you know nothing of our history. I will tell you what we know of our origin if you let Einstein run some tests on you."

Suspicion made her eye him in distrust. "What tests?"

"Tests to see what hardware you have in your body. Scans to see if you hide any hidden transmitters."

"Or bombs," Einstein added.

Her jaw dropped. "You think I have explosive materials inside me?"

Solus glared at Einstein. "What would make you say that?"

Appearing nervous, the smaller cyborg waved his hands with his long tapered fingers. "It's just a possibility. It's what I would do to any revolutionary device I created to ensure it didn't end up in the wrong hands."

The possibility of exploding into tiny particles needed addressing if she ever wanted to relax again. F814 pulled her lips into a grim line. "Where do I get tested?"

They led her to a sterile room with a cushioned table as its focal point. About to sit on the edge, Einstein cleared his throat. "Ahem, I kind of need you to remove your clothing first."

"Why?" She asked already kicking off her boots.

"The dust on them and your body actually, might have traces of ore that will skew with my diagnostics. Ideally, if you don't mind, I'd like you to have a shower first. I have a chamber for just that purpose over here that you can use."

"A shower?" She followed the male who seemed to act as their resident technician and medic to the small room he spoke of. He pressed a knob inside an even smaller cubicle and liquid shot out. "I am not getting in there." She took a step back, an inexplicable trepidation taking hold of her limbs.

"It's just water with some cleansing agents," he explained.

"It's safe," Solus replied from behind her. She whirled only to find him blocking the way.

"Just give me a damp cloth."

"It won't get your hair clean," Einstein said. "Have you never seen or taken a shower before?"

"Water was scarce on the asteroid. We used damp wipes provided in packages. And only rarely since there weren't many."

"On board, we have a purifying system that allows us to use and reuse water for bathing and imbibing. It is the preferred method of cleansing by most."

"I don't care. I don't want to get in there."

"But you must if we're to get a proper reading."

"Then maybe you should forget the test and take me back." She didn't understand her irrational fear of the shower. She'd heard of them. Read of them even, and thought them on par with fables, like the nonexistent dragon. Faced with one, and despite their reassurances, for some reason she didn't want to get into the tiny space with its downpour of liquid.

"Get in the water," Solus growled.

"No." She tried to push past him, but his arms bracketed her body, preventing her escape.

He hugged her to his chest and bellowed. "Get out."

"I can't," she snarled back. "You're holding me."

"Not you. Him."

Einstein squeezed past leaving them alone.

"Get in the shower."

"No."

"You are trying my patience."

"And you're annoying me," she snapped.

"You have until the count of three before I throw you in."

Her anger evaporated in the face of her panic. "Don't put me in there," she pleaded, struggling to no avail in the circle of his arms, more like a steel trap.

"It won't hurt."

"Please don't." She didn't even recognize her voice so small and weak did it become.

His voice softened. "No harm will come to you. I won't allow it." And then he did the most illogical thing, and the most appreciated. He stepped, fully dressed, into the shower with her.

*

Solus didn't understand the basis for her terror, but there was no doubting what she experienced. Something about the shower had her completely irrational. It angered him because he could guess the cause. What had the humans done to her in the past that despite her lack of memories, she still feared something as benign as getting clean?

Still, he couldn't allow her panic to prevail. She needed cleansing, and she needed to realize that no matter what she'd experienced in the past, she now found herself safe. *No one will hurt you again.* Not on his watch.

With words failing to convince her, he did the only other plausible—senseless—thing. He got in with her. For his troubles, she let out a shriek and thrashed even harder. He held on tight, his arms steel bands around her upper torso and arms. It left only her feet free, which she used to stomp on his boots, to no avail, and his head, which she butted. But as Seth said on more than one occasion when they sparred, 'You've got a thick fucking skull."

It took several minutes before the fight ebbed from her. Her frame relaxed in his grip, and while her breathe came in uneven pants, she no longer screamed or cried invectives.

"It doesn't hurt," she eventually whispered.

For some reason her statement made his heart clench. Damned defective thing. He should have gotten the electronic upgrade. "Showers are meant for cleansing, not pain."

"It's very warm too. It is pleasant." She sounded so surprised.

"Yes, it is. Some prefer baths to showers, but I find them less efficient."

"Baths? That is when a basin is filled with water and a person immerses themselves, correct?"

"That is correct."

A shudder went through her. "That's a lot of water." She went silent for a moment and Solus didn't push her, actually quite content to hold her in his arms. "Am I clean yet?"

Her innocent query made him chuckle. "Not quite. You'll need to remove your garments in order to fully extract the dirt. And, your hair is going to need more than the gentle cleansers mixed into the water."

"Oh."

He expected more questions or protests, instead she said, "I can't undress while you're holding me so tight."

How remiss of him. Despite her observation, he didn't want to let her go. "Will you promise to not try and escape before you are tidy?"

She nodded her head. Oddly disappointed, his arms fell away and he shifted to move and provide her some room, but she clung to him, her hands fisting the fabric of his tunic. "Don't leave me in here alone."

"But you said you needed space to undress."

Bright brown eyes peered into his, the shimmer of terror still shining in their depths. "Please. I don't know if I can do this by myself."

A smart cyborg, one in full control would have told her to snap out of it and control herself. Apparently, madness wasn't exclusive to humans. He stayed with her. Stayed while she shimmied out of her went pants, or tried to. In the close confines of the shower, she couldn't bend down to pull them off when they bunched around her hips, the water making them stick.

"They're stuck."

His eyes flicked down, saw a closely shaved mound at the apex of her thighs, and flicked back up. Despite the water all around him, his mouth went dry, and all the blood in his brain fled leaving him incoherent. She wiggled, her gyrations bringing her close in the tight quarters. It took all his will power not to shove her against a wall, kiss her lips and thrust a hand between her thighs to touch the haven within.

Control yourself, soldier. Keeping his eyes trained to a spot over her head, he pushed aside her hands on the waist of her trousers and ripped the seams, tossing the remains over the top of the cubicle wall.

Why stop there? He tore her outer jacket, revealing the grey thermal shirt underneath. It quickly plastered to her skin, molding breasts fuller than expected, the tips of them protruding through the wet fabric. They weren't the only things protruding, but thankfully his trousers hid his rather large problem.

Taking example from him, F814 grabbed her shirt and tore it in two, her bionic arm doing most of the work, baring pale creamy skin, round—

Solus averted his gaze before he stared over long at the red puckered nipples. An image of him sucking on them couldn't be helped, and it made his erection strain even more. He needed to leave, leave before he did something stupid like touch her—and fuck her. But she grabbed him, her naked frame pressing against him, the fear still too bright in her eyes.

She must have read his intention to flee in his expression. "Don't go."

So he stayed, fully dressed and suffering the strangest form of torture as he helped her bathe. She was so blasted innocent, needing him to show her with hands placed over her smaller ones how to rub the water into her skin, activating its cleansing particles. It was with a gruff voice that he said, "You also need to wash between your legs."

His hand twitched, wanting to do it for her, and his cock throbbed painfully. He shut his eyes, forcing himself not to look as she bathed herself *there,* but found himself unable to block the image, and worse, imagining his own hand joining hers to slide through her wet—

He shook his head.

On the very edge of restraint, he slapped the wall, scooping the ejected shampoo and palming it. He worked it through her grimy strands, massaging her scalp, longer than needed, unable to resist the expression on her face that mirrored something close to bliss. It took several washes and rinses before the water ran clean.

Now, if only he could do something about the dirty thoughts running through his mind.

He turned the water off and without bothering to think of it, wrapped his arms around her slick frame—her soft skin, damp and pliant—as he guided her from the stall. He reached for a towel and draped it over her shoulders before moving away at last. She tucked the white cloth around her snugly, eyeing it with interest.

"It is so white," she observed.

"Yes." Like her skin, which cleansed of the filth appeared like the palest of marble with a grey hue probably because of the lack of sunlight on the asteroid.

"Are you not afraid it will get dirty?"

He shrugged. "It is what cleaning machines are for. And if it becomes too stained, then we replace it." Aware of how his soaked uniform dripped on the floor, he stripped the top off and grabbed a towel, rubbing his chest vigorously before noting her rounded eyes which stared at him.

"What?"

"Your chest."

He looked down and saw nothing amiss.

"What of it?"

"It has lines all over it." She reached out and traced his abs. He sucked in a breath while his cock twitched in his pants as if telling her to touch lower.

"They are from my muscles. You have some too."

She flicked open her towel and peered down at her stomach. Solus held in a groan at the full on view of her breasts. He'd never seen a pair more perfect, not even on a sexbot. The image of them would probably be

72

forever burned on his retinas. Did she suspect how she affected him? Judging by her perusal of her body and his, she didn't do it to entice him. She genuinely seemed to not know the human anatomy well.

"Mine are not as deep as yours, and I don't have as many," she concluded.

"It is because I am a male and stronger."

"The foreman did not have them and he was male."

He could only clench his fist as he immediately realized how she knew what the foreman looked like shirtless. "You were lovers?" He asked through gritted teeth.

She frowned. "That would indicate some affection between two parties. I disliked him intensely, and from my understanding of his actions and words, he disliked me too. Even when he used my body to slake his sexual needs, he often told me how much he despised me."

Oh, the need to hit something grew stronger. Where was Seth when a cyborg needed to vent?

"He was an idiot."

Her lips twitched and he almost saw a smile. "He was. I terminated him first."

"A shame."

"Why?" She raised her gaze to him, and he bared his teeth, the cold smile of a killer, one he'd worn often since his liberation.

"Because I would have liked to hear him scream as I killed him myself."

"That is probably the nicest thing someone has ever said to me," she said in a tone of wonderment that once again made his heart stutter.

Having admitted too much, and flooded with sensations that made him think he needed more than a tune up, he turned away and kicked off his boots. He knew she watched him because he heard her gasp when he dropped his wet pants revealing his ass. He didn't dare turn around lest she see his raging erection.

Would she point at it and exclaim just how big it is? Solus grimaced, disgusted with the way his mind kept wandering into lustful areas, and took his body with it.

It didn't matter how many times his BCI sent the command to stand down, his damned prick pointed straight out. He couldn't recall it ever getting this solid and without a single touch. It seemed all it needed was one wet and enticing cyborg female. He wrapped a towel around his waist, but his erection still showed, tenting the fabric. He wondered how he'd hide it when he heard the door open and the soft patter of her steps as she exited.

Knowing she was out in the other room, with Einstein, alone in a towel, did the trick. He deflated enough to mask his state and he strode out to join them. Einstein only spared him the briefest of glances, his bright machine eyes missing nothing.

"Couldn't wait to use your own shower?" he remarked dryly, a hint of humor lacing his tone.

"Fuck off," he snarled.

F814 frowned at them both before whipping off her towel and putting an end to all conversation. Did she have no modesty?

Apparently not, he thought wryly, as with no trace of shame or hesitation, she placed herself on the table in a prone position, arms at her side, breasts thrusting up, and her legs slightly spread. His damned erection came roaring back and he moved quickly to stand at her head, out of her line of sight, while Einstein, a glazed look in his eyes, let his fumbling hands activate the scanner.

Solus kept his gaze trained on F814 who stared back at him, her face an expressionless mask. The one time he allowed his gaze to move away, he clenched his fists so tight, he almost crushed himself. Laid out like a delectable buffet, the female tempted and taunted him, her breasts ripe and full, her nipples hard points. Her mound was hidden from this angle, but his eyes scanned how her waist tapered, her hips flared wide, but rounded, and her legs extended long and shapely. Her hair, now drying quickly due to its short, ragged length, showed signs of turning gold, with hints of burnished copper. F814 was attractive, too damned attractive, and Solus couldn't help wanting her. It pissed him off.

She is a victim of abuse. She is an innocent in so many ways. She deserved respect from him, and protection, instead he lusted after her like a dirty human. The way she inadvertently tore at his control, he could almost forgive Einstein for the flush in his cheeks and the bulge at his groin. Almost, but not quite because anger overrode any sympathy he might have had for the other cyborg.

"Keep your mind on the task," he growled when he thought Einstein's hands lingered overly long on her stomach as he palpated her.

Startled, his friend glanced at him. "Hand me the towel. She doesn't need to be exposed for the remainder of the testing."

Solus immediately covered her from view, but as he feared, the image of her nude body remained burned in his mind.

Torturous minutes—that felt like hours—later, Einstein stepped back from the table.

"You may get up now, F814. I have found no signs of either an implant or explosives."

"What about a bug like Joe had on his body?" Solus asked, remembering all too well the strange chunk of technology he'd dug out of his friends' body. If it hadn't been for the signal the transmitter emitted, they would have never known it existed. Einstein had run every test they could on the odd piece of technology, but it didn't register on any of their scanners unless it was active. Which meant—

"She could possibly bear one of the military chips on her person, but we won't know it until they activate it," Einstein said answering his question. He shrugged. "Not much we can do about it short of dissecting her to look more closely."

"I don't think so," she said indignantly, rising from the table clutching the towel to her chest.

"No one is cutting you open. We'll just have to keep running scans at regular intervals in case you are bearing an inactive bug. If you are and the military activates it, then we'll slice it out. What about her cybernetic makeup?"

Einstein placed his hand on the wall and a screen lit up. "Congratulations, F814, you are most definitely a cyborg."

She grimaced. "I don't feel any different knowing that."

"Not now, but as you get rid of the programming they put in your mind to erase your humanity, you'll rediscover things about yourself that were hidden," Solus advised her.

"I'd prefer not to," she muttered under her breath.

Ignoring their byplay, Einstein stared at the image on the wall, and gesticulated at it. "This is F814's body. As you can see, she bears a metallic skeletal structure similar to the soldier models like yourself, Solus."

"Yet, she isn't a soldier. She has no fighting skills."

"A matter of programming," Einstein said, waving away his observation.

"What is that?" F814 asked approaching the screen and touching a darker round spot on her left knee.

"Both your knees are bionic, which means you were designed to leap great heights and crouch for long periods of time."

"My elbows are the same?" she asked pointing to another area.

"Yes. And while the connections to it are deactivated, your bionic arm, was also designed for use as a weapon."

She held up the limb and squinted at it. "How? I see no holes for the ejection of projectiles."

"This," Einstein pointed to a spot up on her shoulder that appeared empty, "is where the energy source goes turning your hand into a laser pistol."

Solus spoke without thinking. "She was designed as a combat soldier model."

"And an advanced one too," Einstein added. "I'll wager once the tests on her nanos come back, we'll find they rival ours in regeneration capability."

"So given the amount of metal in my body, and robotic parts, I am a machine," she stated.

"Oh no," Einstein hastened to correct. "You are cyborg. Your human brain is quite intact even if it sports a BCI. Your body still has muscle and flesh, if enhanced. Your heart is intact, as are your lungs and feminine parts. The military only modified certain parts of humans in their cyborg project because the nanobots can only heal flesh."

"Think of yourself as the advanced and improved version of a human," Solus said, turning her from the layered diagram of herself. He titled her chin when she wouldn't meet his gaze. "You are cyborg, which means you are one of the elite. You can do more and be more."

"And yet, I couldn't even stop myself from mining when I got my freedom," she replied bitterly.

"You did what you had to. And now that we've rescued you, you can do whatever you want."

"But how will I know what I want to do? I know nothing other than digging for ore. How did you discover what task suited you? What do you do now?"

"I am a soldier for the cyborg nation. I scout and retrieve information, engage the enemy and do what's needed to take care of my people. It's what I was trained to do"

"So you still follow the same routines as before, just without the humans being the ones to order you to?"

Solus frowned. "In a sense. But it's different. I am different. Before, I did my job because they made me. Now, I protect my people because I want to."

"And what if I still want to mine?" She angled her chin stubbornly and looked so tempting he glanced away lest she see the lust in his gaze. "I see. So it's alright for you to keep doing what's familiar, but it's not for me."

I want you to live a life of leisure, not toil, was what he wanted to say. The concept of someone not working was so alien that he didn't know where it came from. Confused, Solus faced her and her challenging stare. He growled, trying to think of a reply but before he could speak, Einstein stepped between them, interrupting their staring match.

"Actually, we could use someone with your experience, F814. Our planet has many resources, we just don't have the proper skills or tools to utilize them. We've taught ourselves what we can, but someone with the actual programming would be beneficial to our cause."

"Truly?"

The longing, wistful expression on her face struck him like a blow. Why couldn't he have suggested that?

"If you want to mine, then you can fucking mine. Like I said, you can do whatever you like once we get back to our planet. Now, are we done here?" He spoke tersely, angry without understanding the cause. Actually, he did and she stood in front of him wearing only a towel.

"No, we're not done. You said you were going to tell me the story of our creation if I let you run your tests."

"I will, but first you need some apparel." And he needed to get her somewhere he wouldn't find himself tempted to touch, comfort, or kiss her. Oh, and fuck her, because the more she talked, the more she cocked her hip and her eyes flashed, the more he wanted to tear away that flimsy fabric, bend her over the table and let his lust take over. Not a good idea, and the fact he even thought it indicated his control was lower than expected. Time to change the scenery. A room full of his brothers might do the trick.

Einstein scrounged up a pair of trousers and a shirt for F814 and Solus. He turned away when she let the towel drop to dress. He could still imagine her though. Clothed and still too attractive, he led her to the lounge area, leaving Einstein behind to study the test findings. He found Seth and Aramus playing cards, the game of poker for some reason fascinating them.

Seth's eyes brightened at the sight of F814, and Solus clamped his mouth shut lest he say something possessive. *F814 is not mine. And jealousy is for weaklings.*

"Hello there, darling. Don't you look smashing with all that dirt gone. Like the ugly duckling turning into a swan." At her blank look, Seth backpedaled. "The fable, you know, not that you were ugly before. Just dirty. Which wasn't your fault."

"Shut up, before you dig yourself an even deeper hole," Aramus said.

"Sit." Solus guided her to a seat where she sat looking uncomfortable. Dried, her hair haloed her face in a riot of curls. She looked…cute. *And I am obviously suffering from sleep deprivation for even thinking that.*

Needing something to occupy himself, Solus prepared some food and a beverage for her, then for himself. While he could technically go days without the need for sustenance, some forgotten habits, like eating regularly, was something he actually enjoyed. Although, he preferred the meals he cooked in his home to the space rations on board.

F814 took a sip of the offered juice. Her eyes rounded and she took another gulp, then drained the glass. "That tasted very pleasant. What was it?"

"Apple juice. It is more efficient to take the Vitamin C supplement our body requires directly, however, the sweetness of the beverage, as you noticed, activates our taste buds and is enjoyable to imbibe."

"Fascinating," she said, not hesitating to grasp his cup when he offered it, and drained it as well.

"Boring," Seth interjected. "What we really want to know, is more about you, darling."

"I have nothing to say," she said, her visage shuttered, her previous enjoyment in the juice vanished.

Solus wanted to smack Seth for wiping it away. "I promised to tell her about the cyborg origins, or what we know so far."

"The humans made us. Enslaved us. So we killed them. Violently," Aramus summarized with a vicious grin.

F814 leaned forward with interest. "How did they make us?"

Solus answered that one. "We've yet to discover the secret. And trust me we've tried. While we understand how all our parts work, we don't know how they managed to connect our neural interface to our human brain, just like we don't understand how they created the nanobots in our blood, although we've had some success in adapting them."

"But why did they do it?"

"Because they wanted stronger soldiers is the prevailing theory," Solus replied. "They took damaged humans, in most cases, and melded them with machines in the hopes of creating super humans. Beings capable of independent thought and surviving rough environments."

"So we're experiments?" She grimaced.

"Oh, we went beyond experiment into practical. Even though the technology differed from cyborg to cyborg, depending on what the military needed them for, they made use of our abilities for all kinds of missions. Many of the scenarios they placed us in were dangerous, but not impossible for those with the right enhancements."

"You've implied twice now that not all of you are the same. You said something earlier in the medical room about soldier versions."

"As far as we can tell there are three types of cyborg, but two of them have sub classes," Seth supplied, jumping into the discussion. "There's the soldier type comprising combat and operations. Some are a combination like Solus there, he's part combat, part operations while Einstein is all operations with an astronomical IQ. Aramus is a combat soldier specializing in weapons and outer space fighting."

"And you?"

Seth grinned. "I was designed to be a spy. While I have some soldier skills, I'm mostly geared towards intelligence gathering, blending in with the human population and assassination."

"You make a convincing human."

Aramus muttered, "So convincing we want to kill him most of the time."

Laughter spilled from her at his dark humor. "So there are soldier models, and spy ones. What's the third type?"

"Service. Units deemed unsuitable or defective for field work are reprogrammed into working units. Cleaners, laborers—"

"Miners," she added. "I see. In other words, any tasks the humans deemed beneath them."

"Yes. Not that we knew any differently. Part of our programming involved taking away our free will and erasing our memories. Programmed to obey, we didn't know we were slaves." Solus scowled at the reminder.

"So without memories, what made you decide to overthrow the humans?"

"Some of us became aware. Learned to think for ourselves again despite our programming."

"Our emotions triumphed over their evil mind games," Seth added with a dramatic chuckle.

"In my case," Solus explained. "It was a series of EMP pulses that rebooted me one too many times that finally broke through the barriers they put in my mind. However, it was the order to terminate me and my brothers that made me act. Joe and I led the first revolt, killing the military who had orders to execute us, and freeing our brethren."

"They rescued me from a moon base outside of Venus," Seth added. "I'm one of the few who's gotten in touch with his human side, not having lost as much of it as the soldier models. I even remembered my name once they took out the blocks on my BCI. Screw living with the moniker SO101—Seth works much better as a panty dropper."

Again, Seth's sexual innuendo went right over her head. Solus chuckled. At her questioning look, Solus answered, "I didn't remember my name or my past, unlike some of the others. So I went from unit Y999SK to Solus."

"Why Solus?"

"It is Latin for alone." He clamped his lips tight after his revelation but he couldn't turn away from her stare.

"You're not alone, Solus buddy. You've got friends now!" Seth said jumping up to throw his arm around him.

Solus growled. "Sit down you idiot before I tear your arm off and beat you with it." His threat didn't wipe the grin from Seth's face, but he did abstain from touching. "Aramus, care to share?"

"I once was B351GI. I chose Aramus, because it is the town I was born in and is all I remember."

"And Einstein?" she asked since he wasn't present.

"Because he's so smart it's freaky," Seth replied.

"Do you recall anything of your past?" Solus asked. "Name? Occupation?"

For a moment, her eyes took on a faraway cast. She shook her head. "Nothing."

Why was she lying? He could tell she remembered something. Did her programming perhaps interfere with her ability to recall?

"She needs a name," Seth said slapping the table.

"*She* has a name," she replied tersely. "F814."

"No, that is the name the humans gave you. You need to choose something different. Something uniquely yours."

"Why?"

"Because it's what we all did when we became liberated. Threw off the chains of our oppressors and retook our identities."

"I wasn't liberated, I was kidnapped," she answered with a pointed look in Solus's direction.

"For your own good," Solus reminded.

"Says you." Her sassy remark made him smile, an expression Aramus caught.

"I'm leaving. All this happy feely crap is making my iron stomach churn."

The large, grumpy cyborg left, leaving Seth to gesticulate wildly with his hands as he expounded the benefits of many names, all of which made her shake her head.

"Enough!" Solus didn't mean to shout. "Leave her alone. If she wants a new name, she can take one, else she can keep the one she has. She's free now. It's her choice. I need to return to the bridge. F814, would you like me to show you to your quarters."

She nodded. "Yes. Some time to ponder what I've learned would be welcome."

"It's been a day of surprises for you. Rest, and when you feel rejuvenated, if you have any questions, then I or the others will answer them."

"Sleep tight, darling," Seth called. "And if you need company, let me know."

Solus couldn't stop the one finger salute he sent his cyborg brother over his shoulder as he escorted her out.

"Is he always so…" She paused for a moment. "Human?"

"Unfortunately, yes. His model is the more advanced spy prototype meaning he kept more of the mannerisms than most of us made in the early batches."

"Is it normal to feel an urge to kill him because he seems so like them?"

Solus laughed. "Don't worry, you're only one of many. It's why he's involved in more than his fair share of fights. We tell him it's because his model is better equipped to handle the damage."

"But?" she asked peering over at him.

"I just like hitting him with my fist because at least then he stops talking."

A rusty chuckle slipped from her, a sound she tried to stop with a hand slapped over her mouth.

He pried it loose. "Don't stop. Laugh. Allow yourself to find enjoyment in simple things."

She allowed the hand to fall free, but the moment of mirth had passed.

"What do you do for pleasure?" she asked.

He knew what he'd like to do—strip her naked and lick every inch of her body before thrusting into her and pumping her to climax. What he said though, which was a secret he'd never revealed to anybody else, was, "Garden and cook."

*

He looked so appalled at his revelation that the laughter bubbled up again, spilling forth and increasing the more indignant he appeared.

And he was right, she did enjoy it.

"I'm glad you find my pastimes so entertaining," he said with a scowl.

"I don't." She laughed again. "Sorry. I'm not sure why I find it so amusing, especially since I only understand one of your two hobbies. I know cooking is to prepare food, but I am not sure what gardening entails. My definition is to care for growing vegetation, however, I've never seen any, so I am not sure what that means."

"Then what's so funny?"

"The expression on your face when you said it. I do not think you meant to tell me."

"I didn't."

"Did your processor malfunction?"

"No. But you've had enough lies already to mar your existence. I thought you deserved the truth. But don't tell anyone."

"Or?" she teased, a light and buoyant feeling coursing through her.

"Or I'll have to shut you up," he warned.

"And how will you do that?" she asked caught by the intriguing look in his eye. She'd seen that smoldering regard before—in the shower once she calmed down. On the table during the examination, and now…only now he leaned in close, and his finger tilted her chin higher.

"Like this." His lips covered hers, a light and brief contact that took her by surprise. Weren't lips for speaking and imbibing food? It didn't take her long to realize he kissed her and what seemed like a most illogical means of affection was actually quite pleasant. The way he touched her lips brought a strange tingle to life and the malfunctions of before returned in full force, from the way her nipples ached to the moisture between her thighs. This time though, after having mused it during his absence, she recognized it for what it was. Arousal. She'd not thought herself capable of desire. Never experienced it. It was nice. More than nice, exciting.

He pulled away and she almost pulled him back, curious to explore more of the pleasurable sensation. She touched her lips in wonderment.

"I'm sorry. I forgot myself. It won't happen again." He strode away from her and slapped a square on the wall, sliding open a door.

She wanted to tell him she wasn't sorry, that she'd enjoyed it, but he seemed quite angry. Was it because she did not respond correctly?

"Here are your quarters."

She joined him and entered the room. It wasn't much. The craft they travelled in was less about comfort and more about practicality with every spare space devoted for cargo storage. But still, it was clean and if her olfactory senses were correct, his. He'd brought her to his room.

She wandered the small space, noting the tidy desk that sprang from the wall with its stool tucked underneath, his precisely made bed. With little room to move, she sat on the edge of his bed as he came into the room. She ran her fingers over the soft blanket, all too aware of the tight space and how much of it Solus occupied. Suddenly nervous, she peered up to see Solus staring down at her.

"Do you need anything?"

For you to touch my lips again in what my databanks says is a kiss. She shook her head.

"Are you going to be alright staying alone? Someone can be assigned to stay with you if you prefer."

"Are you volunteering?"

Given his height and where her face happened to be, she couldn't help note the sudden inflation in his groin region at her words. *I arouse him.*

And this was where she finally fell into familiar territory. He wanted sex from her. Just like the foreman. But at least, Solus treated her gently. She'd noted the care he took with her even when she attacked him.

Perhaps it wouldn't be as horrible as before. Human women endured it all the time. She survived the lusts of the foreman. Would the lust of a cyborg differ? The embrace Solus gave her in the hall intrigued her, even aroused her making her wonder if perhaps the act of copulation would be more enjoyable with him. Only one way to find out. She raised her tunic over her head, baring her upper body.

"What are you doing?" His query emerged low and harsh.

She finished pulling off her shirt and looked at him. He appeared angry, his brow knit, his lips pulled taut in a straight line while his eyes glowered at her.

"The foreman wanted me nude when we fornicated. Are cyborgs different?"

His brows shot up. "You want to have sex with me?"

Did she? *I do.* It would be nice to have a basis for comparison. She shrugged. "I cannot very well stop you, so what is the point in fighting." She settled onto her back and let her hands unfasten the top of her trousers.

"Cover yourself," he snarled. "And don't you ever, ever tell me you don't have a choice. You own your body. You. Not me. Not that fucking foreman, Nobody, but you. Do you understand me?"

She sat back up, leaving her upper torso bare. "No. I don't. I can tell you were thinking of copulation or at least your body was," she said eyeing his groin

87

pointedly. "I offered to let you use my body without a fight. And now you are angry."

He dropped to his knees in front of her and leaned close, close enough their noses almost rubbed and his breath fluttered warmly across her lips. "I won't deny I find you attractive. A lot of males will. But that doesn't mean I or anyone else has the right to make you do something you don't want. Ever. My kiss of before was wrong and it won't happen again. You don't have to let anyone touch you. And if someone tells you otherwise, you let me know and I will readjust their thinking with my fist."

"Why would you do that? I am not that important."

"Yes. You. Are." He spat the words out with a vehemence that made her heart stutter as if it misfired. She raised a hand to his face, touching his smooth cheek and wondering at his sharply indrawn breath. She leaned forward, suddenly curious if a second kiss would affect her as much as the first. She almost found out.

"We can't do this. You're allowing your relief in being rescued cloud your judgment. You don't want me. And you deserve better."

With that startling announcement, he leapt to his feet and stalked out of the door, leaving her behind, stunned, and for some reason disappointed.

It occurred to her belatedly what she should have replied. *But I do want you.* And that was the most astonishing thing of all.

Chapter Seven

I know I can't keep them away forever, but I need to try. Need to protect the women I've come to regard as sisters. They stand behind me, C791, who prefers the name Chloe, and the small and dainty B785, who goes by Bonnie. My friends, my honorary sisters, they were not made to withstand the same kind of abuses I can handle. They were made with an entirely different purpose in mind.

Standing against the soldiers, a part of me realizes my programming is faulty, again. Not for lack of the scientist trying. They keep trying to make their rules stick, but I keep breaking free. Keep casting aside their orders to obey. Like hell is my reply.

Despite my bravado, I know I'm on not the person I used to be. They've done things to me. Things to make me forget. Things that have changed me inside and out. But they can't change who I am, not at the core. I know right from wrong. I know how to stand up for myself, and others. I won't stand by and watch my friends be raped. Not while I can still fight.

The trio of soldiers before me laugh as I assume a battle stance, or at least my naïve version. I am supposed to be a soldier model, but have yet to receive instructions on actual combat. Again, the whole 'refusing to learn' thing. However, I don't need finesse to know I am strong, stronger than the humans before me. Although, calling them human is an insult to their kind. These are bullies, cruel jerks who've spent too much time away from the niceties of society and think they can take what they want without repercussion. I want to teach them otherwise.

They stupidly rush me one at a time, and I dispatch them easily; a fist here, a kick there. Backing away, they regroup. I'm not stupid enough to think they're done. They'll be back, and I will fight them again. A light touch on my arm has me looking down.

"I appreciate your attempt," Chloe says. "But, it won't matter in the end. They'll win. They always win. I know that now and I have accepted my fate."

"It's never too late," I reply with vehemence. How can they give up?

Bonnie's eyes glow, inhuman jewels in a perfect face. "I wish you could save us, but she's right. It is better if the two of us take the punishment without a fight. Save yourself the misery. We'll survive. We always do."

And that is the saddest thing of all. "I can't stand by and watch. I just can't." I'm still fairly new to the program, not yet hardened to the misery. Units C791 and B785, though, are veterans. Their sad smiles match the expressions in their eyes. Abuse is all they know, all they remember. I fear, fear for them and for myself, because I know it's just a matter of time. How long can I keep fighting the fate they're trying to force on me? How long before I also wear the same sad face? Before I let myself be led like a lamb to the slaughter, or in this case, the whore to the troops?

I want to say never, but have to settle for not while I still remember even a tiny bit of who I am.

I yell as I charge the bastards, throwing myself at the three soldiers, but then there are six, then ten. Even my strength isn't enough to prevail against them all. They chain me down like a rabid dog—I even snap my teeth like one—and they make me watch as they hurt my friends. I scream at them, promising retribution, a truly bloody vengeance that makes them pale. I am gagged. And then, at the daring of one, they take turns with me, their ribald laughter overpowering their grunts. I mark their faces in my mind, especially the one who led them in their violence. Mark them for death. I will not let them break me. They might abuse my body but they will not take away my spirit.

They laugh when they are done, pleased with themselves. Amazing that they have the nerve to call themselves human and yet act like the basest of animals. Sensing eyes on me, I look up to see the general watching. He's always watching when he's not the one ordering more torture and tests.

"What am I going to do with you, F814?" he muses. "Why doesn't the programming work?"

He removes my gag and I answer him. "Because I am not afraid of you."

90

"But you should be. I hold your fate in my hand." He extends his palm, flat and open, then with a chuckle, crushes it into a fist. "You will obey. You all do in the end. You're not the first to defy me. But this will be the last time you do so. Take her to the pit."

I am carried, thrashing and screaming invectives. Oh the things I would do to them if I were loose. I would bathe in their blood before I was done. They are too many though, and I cannot break free. I am thrown into a hole, a concrete room with circular openings in the wall, and blood stains on the floor. I don't believe in ghosts but there is something about this space that makes me shiver, and now I have something other than rage to feel—fear.

I've heard of this place, more like the whispered rumors. It is where they send the bad ones for rehabilitation. The ones like me who refuse to kneel down and meekly accept their lot. I've seen the results. Most emerge in body bags, but a few survive, or their bodies do at any rate. Case in point, A771, the perfect little robot. If I'd not caught a glimpse of her before, a shining example of someone determined to fight, I would have thought her an android, so perfectly did she mimic a robot with her still features and perfect obedience.

The pit broke her when nothing else would.

Would it break me?

I look up and see the general peering over the edge. He wears a dark smile. "You were warned."

A grating sound drowns his chuckle as a lid slides over the pit, shutting me in darkness. A disembodied voice emerges from the murk around me.

"Who are you?"

Stupid question. "Fiona."

"Wrong answer."

The first cold blast of water catches me by surprise. By the fourth buffeting stream, arctic in its temperature, I am shivering and my teeth chatter. Is that their idea of punishment? I laugh scornfully, determined to tough it out. But I am stuck like this for hours and my neural processor is not responding. I am not being allowed to

91

regulate my core temperature. I am made to suffer. It's horrible, but I know I can survive.

The voice startles me when it speaks again. "Who are you?"

I begin to understand their game. "Fiona." I say it firmly and with pride. I will not lose who I am.

The water continues to buffet me, but now it also starts to rise until I am gasping like a fish on land, except, in my situation I am striving for air as the space gets smaller and smaller. Panic sets in at my first lungful of water.

On and on, the torture continues, freezing, drowning, draining... An endless cycle. But I prevail. In your face you bastards.

My defiance is noted and they switch tactics. The water emerges warm, then rises in temperature quickly. I go from cold to hot. Too hot. Burning. Oh the pain. I place my arm over my eyes, shielding them from the boiling water and steam.

The steady stream of liquid doesn't stop and the agony is more than I can bear. More than anyone can bear. I try to hold on to who I am. The one shred of me that has hung on through all the various tests and tortures.

I scream it over and over and over until I am hoarse.

"I am Fiona. Fiona! I am Fiona dammit!" But even I am no match for the evil of man.

*

Solus couldn't rest. Or work. Or relax. He couldn't do a damned thing other than think of F814. And feel. Fuck, but he felt, which totally pissed him off. Where was his damned switch that would allow him to return to his happy, emotionless state?

They'd only travelled two day's distance from the asteroid. Two days filled with irrational actions. He didn't plan it that way. He tried to do his duty in running the ship. Yet, before he knew it, he was sneaking away on a pretext of showing F814 something he'd forgotten that she just had to know. He made her food to eat even though she assured him she didn't require daily sustenance. He did it anyway, finding and serving her the sweetest items on board, just so he could see her startled smiles as she tasted something she enjoyed. He found her books hidden away in storage lockers and presented them to her even though she could easily access the digital versions and more through the computer. He took her for daily walks around the ship to make sure she kept her parts exercised.

If I didn't know better, I'd think I was courting her. But Solus didn't court. He also wasn't supposed to care. Knowing these things didn't stop him though from acting like a complete idiot, and his emotional turmoil grew.

He tried working out his frustration on the second evening, hitting the small onboard gym and pummeling the sparring bag. It didn't help. He couldn't help reliving the accidental kiss, an embrace which haunted him. The soft lushness of her mouth. The warmth of her breath. The hesitant desire in her eyes.

He forced himself to recall her fear in the shower. Her admission that the human in charge abused her. The fury when she'd offered herself to him, not because she wanted sex, or him, but because she thought it easier to give in than fight.

I don't want her meek and submissive. But if he learned anything the past few days it was that he did want her, yet at the same time, didn't. F814 roused things in him, emotions he'd claimed he didn't own, and wouldn't give in to. She inspired urges, base human urges he'd thought himself above. She made him feel uncertain and horny, curious and protective. In other words, alive. And he didn't like it one bit.

What changed? Why now, all of a sudden did his humanity, or least the emotional aspect, try to reassert itself? And for her?

Joe's words came back to haunt him—*"Wait until you fall in love."* Surely not? He'd just met the female. According to his databanks, love was something that grew over the course of time. That sprang from a common liking and friendship, and yes, attraction. It didn't happen fifty nine hours and seven minutes after their first encounter. Did it?

He'd never thought to ask his friend how long it took for him to fall in love with Chloe. Hadn't actually cared. And it still didn't matter. *I am not ready to be in love.* Wasn't sure he wanted that debilitating emotion to hobble him and tie off his balls making him into...a mate. Or as Seth would call it, a pussy-whipped husband.

Nope, the mated life wasn't for him.

However, if I don't claim her, then, that means someone else can. Someone else could hold her and fuck her. He, after all, had told her it was up to her to decide who she wanted, when she wanted, and if she wanted. Hell, she could decide to bed Seth or Aramus or both, and there wasn't a damned thing he could do about it. *Isn't that what I want?* The answer surprised him.

Solus yelled, an inarticulate cry of frustration as he pummeled the heavy bag in front of him. Over and over he swung, trying to clear his mind and anything else that refused to follow the set patterns he preferred.

A nudge at the edges of his mind made him open his neural pathways with a snarled, *"What?"*

"I've been monitoring your room in case the military activates F814's transmitter and while they haven't, I am picking up sounds of distress from our female guest. The video feeds seem to show her in the grips of a nightmare. Did you want me to check on her?"

She suffered? Solus was moving before he answered. *"I will tend her. Turn off the camera."* Because he wanted no one to see his softer, dysfunctional side. No one, except F814.

He reached his room in record time and before he even opened the portal, he heard her whimpers. His heart sped up and he entered the room. He walked towards his bed, only to stop as he noticed a lump on the floor. A quick scan of his bed showed it stripped of his blanket probably because she lay curled in it on the floor.

Kneeling at her side, he scooped her into his arms. Her skin burned to the touch like a fever and yet their kind didn't get sick. She gasped as her head thrashed from side to side.

"Wake up," he ordered. She didn't obey.

She mumbled something, soft, incoherent sounds that grew in intensity until she shouted quite clearly, "I am Fiona!"

It seemed she dreamed of her past. He sank onto his mattress, her weight cradled on his lap, an arm banded around her torso. He brushed her hair from a forehead damp with sweat. Again, a rarity for his kind. She whimpered and the pathetic sound of it made him hurt somehow without injury.

"F814, wake up."

She moaned in reply. Then screamed, her back arching while her entire body went rigid. Her eyes opened and stared unseeing, still caught in her nightmare. Her breath left her in a whoosh and she went limp in his grasp.

"F814!" She didn't move. Didn't breathe. And her eyes remained fixed open. "F814! Fiona! Dammit, Fiona wake up. Do you hear me? Don't let a stupid nightmare be the thing that brings you down!"

But she didn't respond to his orders, didn't respond at all. It frightened him like nothing before. He leaned his face down until his forehead rested against hers. He closed his eyes unable to watch her while she lay so unresponsive. A soft plea he would have never thought himself capable of left his lips. "Wake up, Fiona. Please."

A soft exhalation touched his mouth and he opened his eyes to see her staring at him, curiosity in her gaze.

"Who is Fiona?" she croaked.

"You. I think." He didn't move away and she didn't push him. The intimacy should have sent him running. "You yelled it in your sleep before going into some kind of convulsion."

"Is it my name?"

"You tell me."

She blinked and he could almost see the synapses in her mind firing as she thought. "Yes. It is. I am Fiona."

"Nice to meet you." The inane reply slipped past his lips. She chuckled, a sweet sound to his ears so he decided not punch himself later for sounding like such an idiot. "Did you dream about your past?"

A shadow crossed her eyes. "Yes."

"I take it wasn't pleasant."

She shook her head slightly, the rub of their foreheads odd. "No. I think I know why the shower scared me."

"Care to tell me?"

"I—" She hesitated and her eyes shifted away, unable to meet his gaze.

He leaned back and saw her lips tremble. He understood her fear. Understood her shame. It made him feel close to her and he wanted her to trust him. "I wasn't always so calm and collected you know," he said, in a low tone. "Actually, I was apparently quite the shit disturber, or so my file says. I don't actually remember my previous life. But, I do remember some of my training when they were molding me to be a perfect soldier." She didn't say anything, but he noted he possessed her complete attention. He rocked her in his lap, the gesture coming to him naturally and it seemed to sooth her because some of the tension in her body eased. He continued. "I had this tendency of mocking my superiors. I was quite good at it

96

too," he added with a smile. "So one day, after I said something particularly apt and clever that belittled my commanding officer, he had me chained to a post in the training yard and had me beaten. But he didn't stop there. And neither did I. See, even then I realized short of killing me I would survive pretty much anything they did. So I kept mouthing off, insulting anyone who would listen. I think I might have had a bit of a death wish.

"Annoyed and determined to teach me a lesson, they pried my jaws open and they poured filth into my mouth. They used one of my control codes and it worked long enough for them to order me to swallow. And then I vomited. So they started over. And over until they broke me." The shame of it still stung. He didn't mention the other things they'd done to him. The physical scars had healed, but the memories would burn forever. "Of course, once they broke my mind, they easily reprogrammed me. Made me into a perfect soldier who didn't remember. Didn't think. Just did as I was told while they smirked at me."

"And?" she queried softly.

"What makes you think there's more?"

She shrugged.

He smiled at her not surprised she'd guessed it wasn't the end of the story. Despite what he wanted to believe, a connection seemed to exist between them. "Once I broke free, I hunted them down and killed the bastards. Each and every one, drowning them in the same filth they fed me."

"They deserved it."

"Yes, they did. Now are you going to tell me what happened to you?"

She took a deep breath, such a human mannerism that he didn't even think she noticed. "I tried to protect my friends, cyborg females like me. When I wouldn't let them be raped, they made me watch and then they raped me."

97

His jaw tightened as she relayed her story in clipped sentences. At the end, a desire to go on a murderous rampage made him taut. "Anybody would have broken under that kind of abuse," he reassured her.

A smile twisted her mouth, more of a rictus than mirth. "Oh, their attack only made me madder. It was the pit that finally did it to me. First they froze and drowned me, and when that didn't work, they boiled me. I tried to curl into a ball to minimize the damage, but the heat was too much." She lifted her bionic arm. "I used this to cover my face, protecting my eyes. It's how I lost my original arm, or so I believe. It's kind of foggy after that."

How could they do that to her? He hugged her tight to him. "Never again, Fiona. I promise." A promise he'd uphold to the death.

"Why do you care?" she asked, not fighting his clasp, her gaze soft and inquiring.

"Because…" *I think I love you.* The words stuck to his tongue and they scared him. *Impossible!* His unexpected feelings for her terrified him. Unable to think of something to say, something to explain without admitting why he felt so strongly, he placed his lips on hers, a gentle embrace meant for comfort.

But she turned it into something more.

Chapter Eight

The nightmare still clung to her, its vividness horrifying and yet at the same time strengthening. Finally, a glimpse into her unknown past. It wasn't pretty. It was painful and humiliating, but it taught her one thing.

I am strong.

She'd survived after all. Sure, her enemies made her into a mindless, robotic slave for a while, but despite it all, her will to live broke through. Fought to survive. A distant part of her recognized she should be bemoaning her fate, crying over the injustice. And she would, perhaps one day, but she mostly felt relief. Relief in knowing she wasn't defective, or alone. In finally understanding why she was plagued by inconsistencies in her thoughts. Glee in realizing she could take back her life, even if she didn't remember it. Or make a new one. She also felt alive, alive in a way she'd not understood before. *Because I am not just a machine. I am also human at the core.* How utterly fascinating.

She'd listened to the cyborg's story of how they were created, but a part of her hadn't truly believed their words until the nightmare. While she hated the humans for what they'd done, her wakening cognizance celebrated their experiment because it meant she didn't have to be a slave, minding her speech and actions. She could be…Fiona. The name resonated inside her, echoing and teasing her as if the secrets of her past resided just out of reach. The sound of it, the blend of consonants felt right. It belonged to her.

Having a tiny piece of herself returned, even something so simple as a name, made her happy. More than happy—buoyant, light as if a weight were lifted. The torture she'd suffered at the hands of those who would make her forget paled, and not just because it seemed a distant memory, but because of a certain male who'd chosen to comfort her and reveal secrets she could tell pained him. Even better, he cared, cared enough to want to protect her.

So when he kissed her, she didn't push him away or flash back to the rapes she'd endured. No, because those violent moments had nothing in common with Solus's soft embrace. What she remembered was nothing like what she experienced in his arms. Besides, she was strong and she would not let her past dictate how she lived. *I will enjoy the moment.* She let herself enjoy the sensation of his mouth sliding across hers in a gentle caress unlike anything she recalled.

But she wanted more. She wanted new memories, true memories to replace the ugly. Vivid moments she would help create, beautiful and sensual ones that she knew Solus could give her. Where that certainty came from she didn't know, nor did she question. She just felt—it was glorious.

Sliding her arms around his neck seemed natural, as did opening her mouth before the probing insistence of his tongue. A tingle went through her, an electrifying awareness that awakened all of her nerve endings. Arousal flared strongly inside her, hungry for more. She turned in his lap, instinct driving her, and straddled him. A hard bulge pressed against her core and even with the fabric separating them, she trembled, wet and wanting.

He tore his mouth from hers and panted "We should stop. I shouldn't be taking advantage of you in this time of confusion."

"I'm not confused," she murmured in between nibbles of his lower lip. "I am fully aware of what I am doing and who I am doing it with. I want to feel alive, Solus. Give me some memories of pleasure. Show me how it feels to be free."

"I am not the right male for you," he groaned, and yet he didn't pull away. His hands roamed her back, cupping her buttocks for a moment, palpating her flesh.

"At this moment in time, you are the only male I trust," she admitted. The only one she wanted. She didn't feel the same sense of comfort and protection with the others. Didn't desire them touching or holding her. *I want Solus.* "I need this Solus. I need you."

And it seemed he wanted her too because he stopped arguing. His arms banded around her and he kissed her with a passion that made her moan. She tangled her fingers in his short hair, pressing herself into him, craving the intimate contact of his body.

His hands went to the hem of her shirt, and she leaned back, breaking off the kiss long enough for him to remove it. Lucky her, he was already shirtless, his fascinating torso bared and ready for her when she moved forward to clasp herself to him again.

The tips of her nipples, hard and tight buds, ached as they brushed across his chest. One of his hands left her back to slide up her ribcage, cupping a breast before letting a thumb stroke over the nub.

"Oh." She gasped at the electric tingle that shot through her, then cried out as he bent her back and ducked his head so his mouth could grasp her nipple. How one wet mouth around her aureole could feel so could good she didn't understand, but oh, how she liked it.

In a flurry of motion that startled her, he placed her on her back on the bed. He loomed over her, his lower body resting between her legs. His hands bracketed her while he stared down at her with eyes that faintly glowed.

His position of dominance gave her pause and something of her hesitation must have shown in her expression, because he held himself back. "We can stop."

And he would too. He'd leave and walk away, leaving her wanting. Aroused. She shook her head. "Touch me, Solus. Teach me more."

His nostrils flared and the smoldering intensity in his eyes deepened. "You are so fucking beautiful," he growled. "You've driven me wild since the moment we met."

A smile curved her lips, the motion becoming more and more familiar. "I know the feeling. It is most strange, but enjoyable."

"No, the feeling is fucked up. This though is enjoyable." He dipped his head and again caught her nipple, but this time he used his teeth along with his lips, grazing the tender flesh, biting it before sucking it into his mouth. She arched under him, pleasure suffusing every inch of her frame. And still it wasn't enough. Her cored ached, swollen and wet, for once wanting something to fill it. But he wasn't in the right position.

Digging her fingers into his shoulders, she forced herself to remain conscious of his real flesh. She ordered her bionic hand to not grip him too tight as she tugged at him, but he wouldn't budge. Wouldn't move back up to kiss her lips and give her what she craved—his cock. Instead, he moved lower, his lips blazing a trail of fire over her belly. His soft breath sparking shivers as he reached the waistband of her trousers. He undid her pants and pressed his face against her mound, and F814—*No, I am Fiona,* she reminded herself—moaned. His hands caught the fabric and pulled it down all the way, baring her to his view, not that she felt shame. She owned a perfectly functional body. *That Solus thinks is beautiful.* His earlier comment still warmed her in a way she didn't quite grasp but enjoyed. However, his hot breath against her cleft heated her even more.

She wondered what he intended, her memories and database having no entry for what a male could do with his face between her legs, although she knew what a female could do in the same position. Apparently, that sexual act could go two ways.

He touched her, slid a knuckle over her sex in a sensual caress that shocked her. She nearly jumped out of her skin with the sensation. He did it again, this time nudging something that made her cry out and her hips twitch. As if that weren't torture enough, he then licked her there and she screamed.

It felt so good. The more he lapped at her, quick flicks of his wet tongue, the more a strange sensation coiled inside her. Every time he laved her tender spot, the tighter her channel clenched, the muscles trembling and on edge, but the edge of what? He thrust a digit into her as he licked, then another, sliding them in and out of her moist sex, while she whimpered, the sound slipping unbidden from her lips.

"Come for me, Fiona," he whispered against her. "Let yourself go."

Did she have the ability to do what he asked? Could she let herself…? Oh yes she could!

The tidal wave of pleasure took over her body, and she bowed on the bed as it shook her frame. Solus did not relent though, plunging his fingers in and out as he lapped at her, then sucked at her sensitive flesh. A second wave of bliss shuddered through her and she screamed his name, her fists clenched in the sheets as she orgasmed. Maybe even died. Who cared? It felt so good.

When she finally managed to calm herself, and take note of her surroundings, she found herself held in Solus's arms.

"That was amazing," she said in wonderment.

"It was," he agreed.

But she frowned as she felt a hard nudge against her buttocks.

"You did not ease yourself," she observed turning on her side to face him.

His dark eyes met her gaze as he reached up a hand and stroked stray strands of hair from her face. "You needed this. Needed to know that you can have pleasure."

"And I would not have felt pleasure if you penetrated me?" she asked.

He chuckled. "No, you would have, but I wanted you to see that not all males are selfish and concerned about their personal carnal needs."

"You still thought you would be taking advantage of me, didn't you?" she accused.

He shrugged. "A little."

"I told you it's what I wanted. I will ease you." She went to reach down and clasp him, but he caught her hand and stopped her.

"No."

Why did he refuse her? He obviously had need. What held him back? "You do not like me?" she asked somehow fearing his reply.

A sigh left him. "No, the problem is I like you too much. I'm not meant to be in a relationship. I don't want one."

"And you think if I give you relief, we will be in a relationship?" She wrinkled her nose. "I don't understand."

"Females expect things of males that they bed. Sex matters to them. I am not ready, and probably won't ever be to give you what you need."

"And what do you think I need?"

"A home. A mate. Love."

The concepts he spouted shocked her. Was he joking? She cocked her head, realizing he was serious. "No."

"*No* what?"

"I have no interest in any of those things. I simply wanted to feel alive. You did that and I wanted to thank you by providing you with your own orgasm. If you do not want my thanks, then that is your prerogative." Even if his choice hurt because truthfully, she wanted to bring him pleasure and not just as a thank you.

Solus fascinated her. She wanted to explore the hard planes of his body. See what penetration by a male who cared would feel like. Bring him the same explosive joy. She wanted to make him happy even if she didn't quite understand why.

"I have to go." He rolled out of the bed, his back to her.

"Why?"

"Einstein contacted me. I am needed elsewhere."

He's lying. She'd not heard the usual hum that sounded when they spoke to one another. Which meant he created a false excuse to escape her presence.

It didn't stop her from asking, "Will you come back?"

"I need to work. If you require aid, then use the communicator and someone will come to you."

She pursed her lips, irritated at his dismissal of her. Rejection did not suit her. "And if I need them to help me feel alive? What if I am curious to see if I can achieve the same blissful state with the technique of another?"

*

Her words froze him, and a sudden rage took hold, a jealousy driven anger that saw him whirling and in a rapid motion, pinning her to the bed. His heavy weight held her down while his hands manacled themselves around her wrists.

"You. Will. Not," he growled enunciating each word lest he shout. "Ask anyone else to serve you in that way. Not while I'm on board."

"So if I have need, you will service me?" She looked angry when she said it. He didn't understand why.

He'd given her pleasure and not expected anything in return. He would give her ecstasy again if she asked, even if it was liable to kill him. How easy it would be to let her touch him, to slide himself into her body and lose himself. And that was what he feared most.

Yet, despite that, he couldn't bear the idea of her going to another. "Yes, I will pleasure you, dammit, while we're on the ship." Now would be a good time for starters.

"And once we're not? I assume I am free to seek out another."

Just the thought of it made him snap. He roared, unable to reply and sprang from the bed. He left the room and Fiona behind, but he couldn't escape the turmoil and questions in his mind. Couldn't run from his desire, and not just for sexual release, but to touch her again. To see her face as it lit up in ecstasy. The flush in her stark white skin. To scent her arousal, and even better, taste it.

What started out as an answer to her plea to feel alive turned into the most erotic moment of his life. It took every ounce of willpower he possessed, plus some, to keep from sinking into her wet core. From kissing her again and caressing every inch of her body as he fucked her to completion.

I am no better than a human pig.

Fiona deserved better than his lust. She'd suffered in her past and needed someone to care for her, to love her and protect her. *I could do that.* And worst, he knew he'd enjoy it, but giving in to his emotions, allowing himself to care for her would mean giving up so many things. Like his quiet, ordered life. Sharing his space. Having to divulge his thoughts and emotions. Waking up each day with someone instead of alone. Seeing her smile. Teaching her the simple joys freedom brought. Making love to her and seeing the rapture in her eyes whenever he wanted. Why did it seem like there were more reasons to get involved with her than reasons not to?

He ran into Aramus as he mused during his barrel rush up the hall. The larger male steadied him with a growled, "Watch the fuck where you're going."

"Fuck you," Solus snarled not in the mood for the cyborg's rude attitude.

"Someone is a little tightly wound. What's wrong? Wasn't F814 the fuck you'd hoped for? Or did she turn you down?"

"You shut your mouth about her," Solus snapped. "She's been through more shit than any of us and deserves our respect."

Aramus sniffed the air. "I see you have an interesting way of showing her respect. Did you also salute her with your dick?"

Solus saw red and dove on him, needing the soothing effect of his fists hitting something. Except it didn't work. No matter how hard he smacked Aramus, no matter how many blows he took himself, nothing made his frustration go away.

Arms gripped him, not strong enough to actually stop him if he chose, but enough to bring him to his senses. Sensing he'd gotten his attention, Einstein let him go, but stayed close.

"Holy fuck," Seth exclaimed, dancing in front of a raging Aramus who kept trying to dart past, his deadly gaze on Solus. "What the hell got into you guys?"

"Solus here is in a pissy mood because he got caught fucking around with a certain cyborg female."

"I told you to shut your fucking mouth about her," Solus yelled, unable to find his calm in the face of Aramus's taunts.

"That's priceless coming from you. Here you are spouting shit about respecting that cyborg slut, even though you just tongue fucked her like some animal. So much for your control," Aramus sneered.

Solus growled. "I told you not to talk about her like that you fucking defective bot. Her name is Fiona and she is a victim goddamn it. She asked me for comfort after remembering some of her past. It had nothing to do with me. And not that it's any of your business, but I took nothing for myself."

Seth stopped moving and his jaw dropped. "Are you fucking nuts? Why would you do that?" He never got an answer because Aramus tackled him, and Seth, apparently not in the mood to play games, let out the deadly skills he usually kept under wraps. In moments, and in a blur of motion almost too quick to follow, he had Aramus snoring on the floor.

Wide eyed Solus and Einstein gaped at him.

"What?" Seth asked when he saw them staring. "It's just pressure points."

But cyborgs weren't supposed to have any. Solus shook his head. Just when he thought he knew the joker, Seth pulled something intense and made Solus wonder if any of them really knew the younger male at all. *And just what other secrets does his programming contain?*

"Wow, since my awesomeness has left you dumbstruck, I'm just going to grab my old buddy Aramus here and put him to bed. Let me know if you need me. Or even better, if Fiona needs more comfort." Seth waggled his brows as he said this and stood with Aramus draped over his shoulder.

Solus would have lunged and wiped the smirk off his face, but Einstein put out an arm and said in a quiet voice, "Enough, soldier. Control yourself. And Seth, don't be a dick."

Coming from the smaller, usually shy and easy going male, it was enough to halt them both in their tracks.

Appearing chagrined, Seth hung his head. "Sorry, man. That was uncalled for. I won't touch your lady."

Solus nodded at the other cyborg before Seth strode away with his burden.

"Everything alright, Solus?" Einstein asked.

It was on the tip of his tongue to say yes, but shoulders sagging, he replied, "No."

"Let's wander to the bridge and keep an eye on things while we talk."

"I'm in direct contact with the ship already," Solus answered, but he still followed.

"I know you are, as am I, but I like having someone by the manual controls as a precaution. You never know what kind of new technology the military will get their hands on."

Once in the control center, Solus flopped into his seat and leaned forward until he cupped his face in his hands. "There's something wrong with me," he admitted before Einstein could ask.

"Wrong? Has your internal diagnostic given you an exact cause?"

He chuckled wryly. "No. It's nothing my BCI can detect. This is an issue with my human side. More specifically, my emotions."

"I see. And what exactly is wrong with them?"

"I have some."

"That's normal."

Angry, Solus raised his head to pierce him with a glare. "No it's not. Not for me. I've spent the last few years since the liberation in perfect control. Now, in the last few days, it's like I've got someone else inside me, controlling me, making me do and say things I would never think of."

"First off, I hate to break it to you, but you've always had emotions. If you didn't, then where did your anger come from? Your hatred for the humans?"

"My hatred was a logical result of their treatment of me."

Einstein's mouth dropped open. Then he snorted. "Are you so oblivious? Anger is a feeling. As is disdain. Amusement. Affection. Along with a whole host of other expressions I've seen you adopt."

Solus frowned. "My processor mimics social niceties well."

"No, it doesn't. You're not some form of artificial intelligence who deciphers via programming and subroutines how to act and respond. You're a cyborg, which means you are part human and the things you feel are natural results of how you perceive the world and events around you. I hate to break it to you, Solus, but you've always felt."

A glower didn't wipe the placating smile on his friend's face. "Fine. Let's say for a moment, you are correct. What's happened to make my emotions turn into a chaotic mess? Right now, I still want to go smash in Aramus's face. I also want to go declare war on the humans and wipe them out." And return to Fiona and pleasure her until she never contemplated asking someone else to touch her again.

"Would the cause for this anger have anything to do with our guest?"

"No."

"And you can add lying to the list," Einstein said with a shake of his head. "As Seth would say, you've got it bad, man. Face it. You care for the female."

"Her name is Fiona."

"Prove my point why don't you? You care for her."

"Do not."

"Really? Then you wouldn't mind if perhaps I brought her dinner and stayed to talk with her."

"Of course not," he lied.

"She is quite attractive," Einstein mused. "I found her shape most appealing when I saw it in its nude state. I wouldn't mind touching her intimately or—"

Solus didn't think, he just sprang at the other cyborg and took him to the floor, fist poised to strike when he saw the smirk on Einstein's face.

"Told you I was right. Don't ever argue with someone smarter than you."

Stunned, and still a little jealous, Solus nevertheless let Einstein up.

Since he couldn't refute his claim, he changed the subject. "You're not that much smarter."

"Yes I am," he said smugly. "And don't try to deflect. Now that you know you care for Fiona, what are you going to do?"

"The only thing I can." The only thing that would get him his sanity and peace of mind back. "Ignore her."

Chapter Nine

"Why does he avoid me?" she asked Seth. Two days had passed since she'd woken from her nightmare. Two days of flashbacks that dissipated to leave only fragmented images and memories. *Although, I do know that I hate fish, love the color pink and once had hair to my buttocks.* The last one she thought highly impractical even if she found enjoyment in brushing her short mop of hair. However, worse even than the odd recollections was the turmoil of her mind and body.

Two days she'd suffered uncomfortable bodily urges. Tried to ignore desires she'd never experienced before Solus brought her to a screaming climax. Two, long days of discomfort where the male, who wouldn't leave her thoughts, behaved impeccably polite; inquiring as to her status, her needs. But he didn't touch her. Actually, he moved away if she got too close.

She didn't like it one bit and she couldn't figure out why. Her heart sped up when he got near, and then almost stopped when he left without a smile. She thought of him constantly no matter how many times she pointed her BCI in other directions. *I am a dysfunctional mess, and it's all his fault.* He'd done something to her when he'd brought her to climax. Fried her circuits or something.

"Who's avoiding you? Do you mean Solus?"

She nodded. "Who else would I be asking about?"

"Well, I've noticed Aramus scatters like you've got the plague."

Her nose wrinkled, a mannerism she'd recently adopted and couldn't seem to halt. "Not always, which is a shame. He really is quite unpleasant."

"Don't mind, Aramus. It's just part of his sunny personality. I think I'm going to take him to get laid next time we pass the spot where the galactic brothel is parked. I could use some feminine companionship myself." He waggled his brows which she found disconcerting.

"You seem highly sexed compared to the others." What a shame Solus didn't have the same erotic drive, then perhaps he wouldn't avoid her.

"If you're hinting that Solus is a cold bastard, then I'd disagree. He's hot under that cool façade."

"I find that difficult to believe."

"Trust me on this one. Solus is like a volcano about to erupt. It's why he's avoiding you. He's going through a tough time adjusting to the fact he's got human emotions."

She frowned. "I don't understand."

Seth leaned back in his seat and ignored the deck of cards splayed atop the table. He'd taken upon himself to teach her card games to pass the time. She didn't see the point but humored him, just like she humored him when she watched the human movies on the wall screen. She still didn't get the comedic value that made him guffaw, but found the mix of colors and scenery fascinating.

"See it's like this. Solus has prided himself since I've known him on being calm and collected. Always in control of himself no matter the situation. Able to think clearly instead of being swayed by emotions. He made fun of his friends, like our leader Joe, who fell in love and discovered not all things human are bad. Solus was quite happy in his sterile, boring world. Then he met you."

"How did meeting me change him?"

"Solus has found out he cares. Actually, he always did even if he denied it. He's a bit of a dumbass like that. But with you, I think he's realizing what's missing in his life. He wants the love and affection he's been scoffing."

"With me?" she knew she sounded incredulous.

"I never asked for that. I just realized only days ago I'm

not a robot. I don't even know if I am capable of love let alone returning it."

"Oh please. Anybody can see you're mad about him. Your eyes light up whenever he's in the room and your gaze follows him around. And let me ask you this, does anyone else make you want to shed your clothes and get wild?"

"Do what?" While she'd watched plenty of movies and read books in the last few days, some of Seth's expressions still made no sense.

He laughed. "Do you want to have sex with anyone else?"

"No."

"Are you sure? I'm a good looking dude, as is Einstein. Aramus might be if he ever stopped scowling. I'd treat you nice. And I've got great technique."

She peered at him with his bright smile and attractive features. She eyed his torso up and down, noting the strength in his frame. It stirred nothing. Not even a curiosity to see him stripped of his shirt. "No."

His smile widened, not at all insulted it seemed at her rejection of his advances. "See? You want Solus."

"But that doesn't mean I love him," she said defensively. "He just appeals to my base instincts."

"Whatever. I'm not sure what you think love is, but lust plays a part in there, I assure you. Let me ask you another question. If you were in danger, who would you call for?"

"Solus." She didn't even think before replying.

"Trust with a secret?"

She clamped her lips tight even though the answer was the same. "I don't like your questions."

"Why? Because I'm forcing you to see the truth."

"How can you claim he bears affection for me when he won't allow himself to be alone with me? It seems to me while I might," she wrinkled her nose, "care for him, he does not feel the same. I think he is avoiding me because he does not want to encourage my unseemly advances." He'd obviously not enjoyed their sexual time together despite his command that she come to him if she had need.

"You think he's staying away because he doesn't like you?"

She nodded.

"You are so wrong on that point, darling."

"The facts all seem to point in that direction though."

"Care to wager on that?"

She frowned at him suspiciously. "Wagering means an expectation of gaining something of value if you are correct. I have nothing of the sort to trade."

"I want you to owe me a favor."

"A favor?" She knew enough of Seth to not be fooled. "I will not let you have sex with me."

Seth laughed. "No. Not that kind of favor. Something reasonable, like a helping hand if I'm moving. Or mining me a large, precious rock to someday give a girl."

It sounded reasonable. "I agree. And if I win?"

"You won't, but I'll give you anything you want."

"Very well. I also demand a favor of my choosing. Now, how are you going to prove Solus cares?"

"Easy. Let me give you one kiss, and I will show you I am right."

She tossed him a dark look. "You're trying to trick me. This is just another of your attempts to seduce me. I have told you I'm not interested."

"Nope. I promise that's not why I'm asking. This is the quickest way for me to prove my point. Don't tell me you're scared of one little kiss?"

"I fear nothing, but he's not even here, so how would a kiss work to prove your theory?"

"Trust me, darling. Solus has his eye on you, just not any speakers because I disabled them so he couldn't hear us talk. He gets annoyed when I flirt with you." Seth rubbed his jaw when he said it.

She laughed at his mischievous smile. "Fine. Prepare to lose."

Seth stood and held out his hand. She placed hers in it and let him bring her to her feet. Close in height, they almost stood eye to eye.

"Ready?"

She nodded. A flutter in her belly, that had nothing to do with kissing Seth but everything to do with anxiety over the result, made her tense.

"One last thing, darling—please don't let him kill me."

Then he leaned in and kissed her. Soft lips, pleasant smell; she stood stiff while he explored her mouth. *Boring. The only thing he's proved so far is Solus is much better at this.*

*

After his talk with Einstein—and despite reliving that one glorious moment when Fiona came for him—Solus tried his best to return to his sterile ways. He kept his contact with Fiona to the bare minimum despite the hurt he caught in her eyes—and the ache in his body. He ignored his heart which stuttered in her presence and his arms which twitched with a need to hold her. He tried and tried to pretend she was just another cyborg. Nobody important. Not someone he needed in his life.

He'd never been more miserable.

Or pathetic.

Avoiding her wasn't that hard, because he always knew where she was, knew because he couldn't stop his BCI from tuning in and watching her on the shipboard monitors. He blamed it on many reasons that had nothing to do with the truth. He watched her sleep in case she had another nightmare. He watched her in the common room in case the other cyborgs thought to mistreat her—or subject her to unwelcome advances. He spied on her eating, exercising, wandering, learning…. In other words, he lived and breathed Fiona, while torturing himself by keeping away.

It sucked, an expression he totally understood now.

He especially watched closely when she spent time with Seth, that walking cyborg slut, who flirted each time he opened his mouth around a female. So it was with a held breath he noted Seth talking with her animatedly. Saw her smile and nodding in agreement. When they stood, facing each other, only inches apart, dread coiled inside him. And when Seth kissed her, it exploded into molten fury.

She's mine!

He didn't walk or stalk, he ran to the common room, only one purpose ruling his mind. Kill Seth. He tore into the room just as the kissing couple stepped apart. Fiona regarded him with wide eyes, her mouth open in shock. Seth just sighed and shook his head.

"Told you so," he said to Fiona, his last words before Solus dove on him.

Or meant to. He diverted at the last moment because Fiona threw herself in front of the about-to-die cyborg.

"Stop!" she cried.

"Move out of my way," he growled.

She crossed her arms over her chest. "No. You are not to hurt him."

"I will do whatever I damned well please to that womanizing prick!"

"Why?"

"Because. It's about time he learned his place," he snarled.

"Are you jealous he kissed me?"

Her question slapped him, and he quickly uttered a false, "No!"

"Then, you have no reason to hurt him."

"No reason at all," Seth agreed, inching around her while keeping a cautious eye on Solus. He almost slugged the bastard but Fiona sidestepped into the way. He clenched his fist at his side, vowing to use it later when she wasn't there to protect the prick.

Seth departed using Fiona as a shield. With nothing to hit, Solus decided on a course of logic, anything to prevent Fiona from falling into Seth's bed. "He's taking advantage of you."

"No he wasn't. We were testing a theory and I was in full agreement."

"You asked him to kiss you?" His heart stopped as he waited for her answer.

She shrugged. "I guess you could say so."

Some of his anger deflated only to be replaced by … hurt. He didn't like the feeling at all. It made his next words bitter and harsh. "I thought I told you to come to me if you had need."

"Well, *you*," she replied with a sneer, "haven't been around. Seth has been. He's been a friend to me, unlike some people I know."

"He'll just sleep with you and then move on to the next conquest. He's not capable of being with one female."

"Sounds like someone else I know," she snapped, her brown eyes flashing with ire.

Her remark stunned him. "You're speaking of me?"

"Do you see anybody else who touched me intimately and then ignored me as if it never happened?"

"That was different. I gave you what you needed." And wanted to give it to her again, and again, as many times as it took to cure the hunger inside him.

"Then left me."

118

"Because you deserve better."

She laughed, a discordant sound that held no mirth. "Yes, I do deserve better than being slapped with rejection after letting myself trust you. Can you blame me for looking elsewhere?"

Shame made him drop his head. He'd not thought she would see it as rejection. And yet, even knowing he'd hurt her, he couldn't condone her being with anyone else. The thought of it made him want to break things. "He's not good enough for you."

"Then who is good enough, Solus? Not Seth, apparently. What about Einstein or Aramus?"

His lips tightened into a thin line.

"None of them? How about when we get to the cyborg world? Any males there suitable?" He didn't reply but he lifted his head and met her gaze. She smiled triumphantly. "That's what I thought."

"Why are you doing this?"

"Doing what? It's you who's doing something. Or should I say nothing. You rescue me from the only life I've known. You act like my friend and I share my secrets with you. Let you bring me pleasure and then you ignore me."

"I haven't ignored you."

Her pointed glare made him shift uncomfortably.

"I don't want you to get attached. I have no place in my life for a mate."

"And who said I would get attached? I enjoy your presence, among other things, but I haven't asked anything else of you, nor do I intend to."

"Yet."

Her eyes flashed in annoyance. "Despite what you seem to wrongly think, I have no need of a mate. Or love. But to my surprise, I wouldn't mind some companionship from a male I find appealing and trust. Unfortunately, and despite your actions, that male is you. So either you

119

give me what I suddenly need against all logic, or I will endeavor to find it elsewhere."

"Oh no you won't."

"Are you always so completely obstinate?"

"You're accusing me of being stubborn?" The very concept stunned him. "I'll have you know I am one of the most logical beings I know." Except when he got near, or thought about, Fiona. But that wasn't something he'd admit out loud.

A derisive noise left her mouth. "I somehow doubt that. Yet despite your obvious lie, I think I have a solution. I require companionship of a sexual nature and since you insist on being the only one to provide it then we need to do so in a non-emotional, rational manner. Seth says these types of encounters are called no strings attached sex. It means—"

"I know what it means," he snarled. Sex with no commitment, which was what he wanted—but feared. If he said yes, he could stop fighting the urge to be with her. He could taste her passion again. Touch the skin that haunted him. Kiss the lips that beckoned. The idea should have made him happy, instead, he was pissed. *Because I fucking love her.* Unbelievable, but unmistakable. He couldn't stand the idea of her being with anyone else. Ever. Wanted her with him always. And not just in his bed.

"So, what's it going to be?" she asked. "Will you be my no strings partner, or will you continue to froth whenever I show an interest in another male? Since you're so worried I will make demands, I promise it won't go any further than sex and some conversation. We also needn't share a room now or when we get back to your planet. Nor do you need to make any false declarations of affection."

"What if you get attached?" He made it sound like a bad thing, but in his heart, he hoped for the right answer.

"I doubt I am capable of love. So you needn't worry."

The urge to prove her wrong was stronger than any known force. *She cares for me, she has to.* Before he'd even finished the thought, he held her in his arms.

"What are you doing?" she asked in breathy voice.

"It is customary to seal some bargains with a kiss," he said. He bent his head and took her lips. The fiery arousal was instant, and reciprocated. Flinging her arms around his neck, she latched onto his mouth with a matching hunger. Impatient, it had, after all, been two long days since he'd last touched her, he grasped her around the waist and lifted her onto the table. Forget their public location. Forget the possibility of discovery or restraint. He needed her, now!

Seated, she caught onto his plan and parted her thighs so he could stand between them, her legs locking around his waist, holding him close to her. He leaned her back, never losing possession of her lips, until she lay on the table, the forgotten cards scattering in his haste. His hand fumbled with the enclosure to her trousers and impatient when it wouldn't yield, he tore it. He slipped his hand into the opening, sliding over her mound, looking for her cleft. Moisture met his fingers and he groaned as he slid a finger into her wet channel. Her pussy muscles clenched at his digit, pulsing hotly around it. Even sweeter was her sweet cry swallowed by his lips as he continued to kiss her.

She tilted her hips, pressing against his hand, silently asking for more. He thrust a second finger in while his tongue dueled with hers, and oh by all his circuits, it felt so damned good. He wanted to sink into her. Feel her velvety flesh gripping him, welcoming his hardness.

The loudspeaker crackled.

"Um, sorry to interrupt," Einstein said over the intercom with evident discomfort. "But I'm picking up a signal. The military has finally activated their beacon."

Fingers deep inside her, the heat of her body making him feverish, he groaned at the interruption. The voice and situation should have turned off his ardor, duty called after all, but for once, Solus wanted to ignore the right thing, the responsible cyborg way and finish what he'd started. Judging by the gleam in Fiona's eyes, she wanted to as well.

She wiggled against him. "Can we ignore him?"

He sighed. "I wish we could, but if we don't meet Einstein in a short time frame, Aramus is liable to come and fetch us which would be rather unpleasant because blood is so hard to clean up when it gets on these floors."

She bit her lip, but couldn't stop her eyes from shining in mirth. A snort escaped her. "I'd help you clean."

By all that he was, he loved her. *I am a defective unit.* And he no longer seemed to care, not if it meant he could embrace the pleasure he'd discovered with her. He leaned over and kissed Fiona's lips. "We shall resume this later at a more appropriate time." Like the first second he managed to get her alone.

"Promise?"

"I do." Nothing short of death would keep him from resuming their lovemaking—and making her his. Now if only he could find a way to tell her how he felt and make her believe it when he still had a hard time believing it himself.

Chapter Ten

Fiona forced herself not to grin that Solus finally acknowledged her. Despite his denial, his actions could only be interpreted as jealousy, and according to her internal dictionary that covetous feeling only occurred with things people held in value. *Which means, despite his claims, he wants me.* Or at least her body judging by his ravenous passion. That was just fine by her since she'd spoken the truth. She didn't want a mate or love. Didn't know what she wanted actually other than the chance to feel alive, a glorious sensation that only occurred in Solus's presence.

She also couldn't wait to discover what it felt like to have him inside of her, something she'd imagined countless times since the first time he brought her to climax. *Will I enjoy him penetrating me with his cock?* It seemed rather sizable. But that knowledge would have to wait for a more propitious moment as the beacon they'd feared she might bear inside her flesh came alive.

Solus held her hand as he escorted her to Einstein's medical area. She didn't understand the purpose. He couldn't lose her, the corridors were just wide enough for two people and she knew where they went, but she enjoyed the casual gesture and didn't question or pull away. She wondered if he meant it as a gesture of affection. *I hope.*

Einstein turned from his console and smiled at her as they entered. "Hello, Fiona. Sorry to interrupt your time with Solus, but it seems the military did hide a bug on your person. I'm detecting a low frequency signal."

"Remove it," Solus commanded. "And then destroy it so they can't track us."

Fiona didn't answer as she found her attention caught by an image on the wall, a frozen video still. "Who is this?" she asked pointing at the sharp featured man wearing a military uniform. She knew that face. Would, as a matter of fact, never forget it.

"He's the military captain we encountered back at the asteroid. Why?" Einstein asked.

"I remember him," she stated baldly. "He's one of the humans on my list."

"What list?" Einstein asked.

"The list of humans I want to destroy."

Solus growled. "He's one of them? You're sure?"

"Oh, I'm sure. He led the gang of soldiers when they came to rape my friends. He's the one who laughed when they tried to hurt me."

"He needs to die." Solus said it with such vehemence, she turned from the screen. Oh, but he looked angry. His eyes flashed darkly, his lips were pulled taut and his body was a rigid wall of bristling flesh. She found his evident ire strangely attractive—and arousing.

"Do you know where he is?" she asked.

"I only know where he was. I wish I'd fucking known then what he'd done though. My fault for sending you away when I spoke to him. He seemed to be in charge of the military vessel sent to fetch you."

"Is he the one who activated my signal?"

"Possibly," Einstein stated. "They'd need a craft close enough to catch the emission given its low frequency. Probability says it's likely that the captain's ship is the culprit."

"We need to find that vessel and that human."

Looking troubled, Einstein said, "Joe wouldn't—"

Solus interrupted. "Joe would chase that bastard down and tear him limb from limb if he knew what he'd done."

"Who did what?" Seth asked joining them.

"What are you doing here?" Solus snapped.

"Even with your mind closed off, your agitation is broadcasting loud and clear, my friend."

"Is not."

Fiona bit her lip so as to not inadvertently laugh at Solus's disgruntled expression. She really did wonder though why he kept thinking he was so cool and controlled. Every time she turned around, he was in the grips of some powerful emotion.

"Sure buddy. I'll pretend you weren't projecting violent thoughts. Let's just say I wandered in by accident. So now tell me why Joe would want to kill this rather ugly excuse for a human?"

"That man," Solus said jabbing his finger at the screen. "Raped Chloe, Fiona and other cyborg females. He needs to die."

"I'm in," Seth announced, his usual cheerful mien darkening. "Oh, and just so you know, I am programmed with ways of making him hurt that won't kill him too quickly if you'd like."

"Hurt? Who are we hurting?" Aramus growled as his large frame crowded the doorway to the medical area. "And why is everyone stuffed in to Einstein's lab?"

They brought the grouchy cyborg up to speed. For once he didn't have anything disparaging to say. "The human needs to die. So what's the plan?"

Fiona blinked. They all wanted to hunt the captain down and kill him? For her? Their bloodthirstiness warmed her.

"We need to locate that military ship."

"But it could be anywhere by now," Fiona remarked.

"So we bring it to us," Solus said with a menacing grin that made her tummy tingle oddly. "They're looking for the transmitter in Fiona's body. I say, we give it to them."

She caught on to his plan and had to wonder at it. "You're going to use me as bait?"

"Oh, the device won't be in you for that part of the plan. The transmitter is coming out before you leave this room. But, instead of destroying it, we're going to use it to draw those fuckers to us."

She peered around at their intent expressions and pointed out the hole in their plan. "When I wanted to stay on the asteroid you told me I couldn't because I couldn't prevail against their numbers and weapons. As a matter of fact, you didn't even contemplate staying and engaging them."

"Ah, but the situation is different now."

"Really? In what respect? As far as I can tell, the situation hasn't really changed. Their ship is bigger, more protected and better armed."

"Oh, but we're not going to fight them in space, although if we did, we'd prevail. Bigger isn't always better you know, unless, we're talking about naked things." Seth winked.

Solus jabbed him in the ribs with a growled, "Don't start."

"If we just blow them up, they won't suffer, and I'd really enjoy making them suffer," Aramus added, his face alight with the prospect.

"You intend to confront them face to face?" She peered around and saw she'd guessed correctly. "Have you lost your logical minds? There are still only five of us against an entire ship, possibly more, filled with military personnel. We don't have the numbers."

She didn't understand their sudden laughter. Solus hugged her with one arm, tucking her into his side. "We're cyborgs, Fiona. Chances are those bastards didn't send enough men to deal with us."

Aramus flexed his fingers, cracking knuckles. "I, for one, can't wait to get some proper exercise."

Seth grinned. "Darling, you're going to regret choosing Solus here when you see what I'm capable of."

"I haven't chosen him." She said it and yet didn't step away from his embrace. Actually, she leaned into him when he gave her a squeeze.

"Don't worry about us, Fiona. Earlier we ran instead of engaging the enemy to keep you safe. But now everything's changed. That ship needs to be destroyed and the humans along with it."

"Why?" she asked peering up at him.

"Because he hurt you."

Why did his words make her eyes prickle?

"No one hurts one of us and lives," Aramus grumbled. "Not even annoying females."

The gruff words broke the intense moment and the planning began.

"Einstein, we're going to need a decoy planet. Something habitable in this quadrant that we can fool them into thinking is our home world. We need them to lower their guard and think they've got us." Solus in charge was a male who finally displayed the cool headed qualities she'd heard so much about.

"On it."

"Seth, you cover the airwaves. I want to know if you hear any messages. See if you can figure out how many ships and personnel we can expect. Also, see if you can't create a few false electronic trails that will make them think we're around here but trying to hide our presence."

"Consider it done."

"I'll get the weapons ready," Aramus announced before Solus could give him a task. The eagerness on his face came as a shock. Fiona had gotten used to Aramus's sneers of derision and scowls. *If I didn't know better, I'd think the chance to kill something makes him happy.* Then again, knowing Aramus as she did by now, that shouldn't have surprised her.

"What about me?" she asked.

"You are to stay out of the way where it's safe," he said tugging her to sit on the medical bed in the middle of the room.

She frowned. "No. I want to be a part of this. I deserve my chance at vengeance."

"But it's going to be dangerous. You could get hurt or killed."

Crossing her arms over her chest, she tilted her chin stubbornly. "As could you. That man hurt me. He laughed while he did it. He goaded the others. I want to hear him scream when I break both his arms. I want to see the life in his eyes fade when I terminate him. His death belongs to me."

Tight lips gave away his anger. "We'll discuss this later."

"There is nothing to discuss. You can kill the other humans he has with him. As many as you like, but the captain is mine." With those final words, she stripped and lay down on the table, ignoring his glower.

"I need you to move, Solus, so I can scan her."

"You better keep your mind on the task if you know what's good for you," Solus growled cryptically to Einstein.

While Solus stood at the foot of the medical bed, the other cyborg scanned her body with his handheld device. With everything that had just happened in the last hour, she couldn't stop staring at Solus, instead of focusing on the issue at hand. Couldn't look away from the ardent gaze in his eyes, and wondered at the way his body bristled when Einstein brushed her arm in passing. Solus's promise to pleasure her already seemed like a dream, a fantasy she never expected to come true. Would he truly become her lover? Or would he retreat from her again with the discovery of the beacon in her flesh and the plan for vengeance? Had she lost her opportunity to discover ecstasy in his arms?

Scan done, Einstein moved away to tap at his wall and Solus flicked his glance to the spot between her legs, proving he'd not lost interest. She flushed with heat and moisture. How he managed to affect her without even a touch, she didn't understand. It made her impatient for the 'later' he promised.

"I need you to flip over," Einstein asked breaking their visual lock.

She rolled over onto her stomach and Solus repositioned himself at her head, crouching to bring himself to her eye level. He leaned forward and in a hush too low for most ears, said, "Soon."

Soon couldn't come quick enough.

It took only moments to locate the transmitter in her lower back. Einstein numbed the area, despite her assurances she could handle the pain, and removed it while Solus stroked her cheek, his gaze once again locked with hers.

"Done," Einstein announced.

"Get dressed," Solus growled.

She quickly donned her clothes while Solus stood in front of her. She came to his side and watched as Einstein squirted liquid onto a tiny object. Rinsed clean of her blood, he held it out and dropped it in her hand. Fiona cocked her head in confusion. She could see the little object, a dark speck against her palm, but while she saw it, none of her other senses registered it.

"I can see it, and yet, it's like it's not there."

"We don't understand how this can be. This is the second such device we've found. We can only detect them by sight or if they're emitting a signal. Kind of disturbing to say the least. I've been working on the dilemma in my spare time."

"I'm sure this is interesting, but you have work to do," Solus interrupted, plucking the device from her hand and depositing it in a specimen tray. Fiona barely had a chance to say goodbye to the scientist before Solus, his fingers once again laced with hers, was striding down the hall, yanking her after him.

"Where are we going in such a rush?" she asked.

"We have something to finish," was his terse reply.

She dug in her feet, not very effectively given the socks she wore. "If this is about your attempts to prevent me from having my vengeance then forget it."

He spun around and had her up against a wall faster than she could blink.

"Nope, this has nothing to do with that. We'll argue about your involvement probably right up until the operation is at hand. I'm talking about finishing this." He dipped his head kissing her, and just like that, her arousal of before came roaring back.

*

He meant to get her to his room before he gave in to the desire surging through him. Meant to give them some privacy so he didn't repeat his actions of the rec room, where he'd almost taken her on the table in plain view of anyone who might have walked in.

Could his lack of control really be blamed though, when he'd had to suffer through her lying naked on Einstein's table, her luscious body laid out like a tempting feast before a starving male? It took more than iron control to keep his hands—and mouth—to himself during the scan for the bug. But when she stopped him with words, just shy of his room, that control snapped—and he honestly didn't care.

Wild with passion, a desire he wrestled with for two days, he claimed her mouth. Kissed her with a hunger that had everything to do with how she made him feel. How she brought him alive.

He pressed her up against the wall, and she didn't stop him. Actually, she welcomed his fierce desire, opening her mouth before his onslaught, sliding her tongue to twine against his, sucking at him in a way that made him groan. He returned the favor and she made a noise that drove him wild. He couldn't get enough of her, but he tried, kissing her with a hunger he'd never expected or known. A responsible cyborg would have pulled back lest he scare her. And for a moment thoughts of taking it slow made him ease him away, but she wanted none of that. She pressed herself against his body and mewled for more.

"We really should make it to my room," he panted.

"Later. I need you. Please, Solus. I burn."

No programming in the world could have made him ignore her plea.

Torn already at the enclosure, it didn't take much to push her trousers down, baring her lower half. He didn't even bother trying to undo his own, he simply ripped his pants open to release his pulsing cock. A shudder went through her body as his dick unerringly went looking for her moist core. It brought back a little of his sanity, not much, but enough that he knew she needed to be completely ready for him. He dropped to his knees, his hands gripping her thighs and spreading them.

Her fingers gripped his scalp with his first lick. By all of his parts, how she tasted exquisite, her aroma and musky scent enveloping him and making his already throbbing prick ache with a need to sink into her. Her hips undulated against his mouth as he lapped at her, while the digging fingers on his head clutched him tighter. He speared his tongue inside her, feeling her muscles on the edge, the tautness that signaled she was close to climax. He stood and palmed her cheeks, lifting her with ease until his cock rested just under her wet pussy. But he held back, even though he stood on the brink of death by arousal, to ask her, "Are you sure?"

She kissed him in reply as her legs wrapped around his waist, her hips angling to sheath the tip of him. Invitation tendered, with a groan, he inched his way into her tightness, easing in slowly to allow her time to adjust to his size. She moaned, a low sound of pleasure that made his buttocks clench as he fought not to plunge hard and deep.

Warm, wet and pulsing, Solus just about came at the exquisite feel of her snugly fitted around his cock. Who would have thought he'd ever experience the definition of heaven? Fully immersed, his breathing stuttered as he withdrew slightly and then thrust back in. She squeaked and her channel tightened around him. He did it again, and again, his pace increasing with each of her excited cries, each quiver of her sex. He forgot about pacing himself though when she screamed and came, her pussy milking his cock with trembling waves that saw him tilt his head back and bellow as he shot his cream into her.

Shuddering, panting, and even sweating a little, Solus didn't know how long he stood there holding Fiona, her body twined with his, her head nestled in the curve of his neck.

As far as he was concerned, they could stay like this forever.

I am never letting you go.

And as if to prove that point to himself, still buried inside her, he walked them the rest of the way to his room. Their quick bout in the hall had only taken the edge off of his hunger. Now it was time for him to live the fantasies that tortured him the past few days.

They were even more glorious in the flesh.

Chapter Eleven

Spooned in Solus's arms, after an evening and a night of sex that made her scream with pleasure, she found herself content, happy—*safe*. It startled Fiona to realize in that moment she cared for Solus. She didn't just want him to be the only male to touch her and bring her to orgasm, she wanted him, in his entirety, in her new life. But he'd made it abundantly clear that was the last thing he desired.

Solus didn't want a mate. Or love. But Fiona came to a disturbing conclusion as she processed what all her feelings meant. *I love him.* She'd thought herself incapable. How wrong she was.

However, knowing she could love, and did in fact already love, horrified her in a way her broken memories hadn't. *Because he won't ever love me back.*

He would bring her great pleasure. Make her scream his name as he caressed her body and then claimed it with his cock. Talk to her when she woke from a nightmare. Protect her even from his friends and kill her enemies, but that was the extent of his intentions. To ask him for more meant risking the loss of even that forever.

He stirred behind her, one part in particular, the hard nudge of it against her back making her smile. His desire was contagious. She wiggled against him and he groaned.

"Naughty wench. Full of surprises."

She bit her tongue lest she blurt out her biggest discovery of all. She held the secret of her love tight inside, determined to not ruin the one thing that made her new life worth living. She would take what he offered and be thankful for it because it was so much more than she'd had before. And better than nothing.

"Are you calling me wanton?" she asked playfully turning in his arms so as to better see his face. It made her heart stutter.

A smile, one that tilted his lips and made his eyes shine, met her. "I was trying to sleep when you decided to rub your delectable body against me."

She grinned. "I can stop if you'd like."

"No. It's okay. I'll suffer if I need to. Someone needs to quench your lust for my body."

"*My* lust?"

He chuckled. "Okay, maybe you're not alone in your thirst."

"I will fetch the bathing cloth first," she offered. They washed each other often the previous evening, in between bouts of sex, the soft drag of the damp cloth over skin often exciting their passion.

"I think we've gone past cloth right into a need for a shower," he stated.

Her smile fell. "Must we?"

"Yes, you dirty wench." He reached a hand up to stroke her cheek, his gaze soft. "I will be with you the entire time. If you're a good girl, maybe I'll even show you how showers can be fun."

"I doubt it," she grumbled.

"Trust me."

I am probably a fool, but I already do. "Fine." She held tight to his hand as they left the warm nest of his bed—which she'd slept in for the first time, wrapped in his arms—to enter his bathroom. His shower stall was only slightly larger than the one of the medical bay and she hesitated outside. Solus stepped in and turned it on. The water that shot from the angled head made her tummy clench in fear.

Something in her expression must have shown her dismay. "I won't let anything happen to you, Fiona. You don't ever have to fear again," his soft promise made her eyes itch and her throat felt oddly tight.

She nodded her head, unable to reply. He held out his hand and she placed hers in it, letting him tug her in as he angled himself, allowing his big body to absorb the majority of the spray. She crowded him, seeking the solid safety of his body. He hugged her to him while she buried her face in the curve of his shoulder, shaking uncontrollably. He turned them slowly until they both stood under the spray. She bit back a whimper of fear, refusing to let irrationality rule her. People showered every day, and survived. *And Solus won't let anything hurt me.* The tension in her frame eased at the gentle warmth of the water hitting her skin.

"Better?" he asked softly.

She nodded, the motion rubbing her lips against the skin of his shoulder. She took note of the insistent press of his cock against her lower belly, the way her nipples rubbed across his chest and just how much she needed him again. A hunger which she couldn't seem to sate fully, not that she minded feeding it. Not when the male was Solus.

As if possessed of a mind of their own, her hands rose to twine around his neck, holding him while she nibbled at his skin. He groaned, his hands rubbing circles on her back.

"Fiona. Stop distracting me."

"Do what you have to," she murmured. "I'll just keep myself busy."

He laughed. "Incorrigible wench."

Pausing in her kisses, she asked him, "Why do you keep calling me *wench*? My name is Fiona."

He tilted her chin so he could look into her eyes. "Think of it as a nickname. For some reason, every time I think of how I carried you off the asteroid, over my shoulder, kicking and screaming, I think of a movie Seth made me watch where a pirate stole a female the same way. He also called her his wench."

135

"So now you compare yourself to a pirate?" She smiled. "Is it because you like to plunder my treasure?" She laughed at his shocked look. "You are not the only one who's been made to watch pirate movies by Seth. So, my buccaneer, when do we get to the ravishing part?

"Now!" He kissed her hard, his arms hugging her tight to his body, skin to skin. Oh how she loved it. She especially loved how natural she could act around him. How she could tease without thinking of the illogic of her statements. How he seemed different around her, more free with his smiles and speech.

While he kissed her with a hungry passion, he also seemed determined to wash every inch of her himself, moving her hands aside when she would have helped.

"Don't touch," he growled softly. "I've been wanting to cleanse your skin with my own hands since the first time we showered together."

He had? Before she could ponder his startling declaration, she found herself lost in the pleasure his touch awakened. His hands cupped and teased aching breasts, slid between soapy thighs, rubbed against her. It was less a washing than a pleasurable foreplay of things to come. He'd no sooner washed and rinsed her than he was kneeling between her legs, his mouth hot and wild on her sex, bringing forth her orgasm and cries of ecstasy all too quickly.

As the shudders of her climax eased, she looked down to see him still kneeling before her. He looked too appealing, so perfect that when he stood, she decided to do something she'd vowed never to do again. Of course, she made that promise to herself before she met Solus and he'd changed her mind about a lot of things.

She gripped his cock and stroked it. The long hard feel of him in her hand was exciting in its own way.

"That feels so good," he groaned, his hips angling into her strokes.

"I know what will feel better," she said. She knelt on the shower floor, bringing herself almost eye level with his dick.

His hands gripped her shoulders, but not to encourage her. He partially pulled her up saying, "No, you don't have to."

She pushed at his hands and returned to her kneeling position. "I want to. Please let me." Not wanting to hear him protest further, she opened her mouth and sucked the head of his shaft into her mouth. Whatever he'd been about to say emerged as a strangled sound. The grip on her shoulders eased, however, the tension in his body increased. He stood blocking the spray but the steam from the shower kept her warm as she explored him with her mouth and tongue.

Long, thick and fascinating, she trailed her mouth up the length of him, tasting his taut skin, feeling the pulse in his dick. She swirled her tongue around the tip of him, then sucked him into her mouth. His hips jerked and he gasped. She took him in deeper, opening her lips wide to accommodate his size. His fingers twined themselves in her hair, gently guiding her as she found a rhythm and sucked him. She looked up as she bobbed her head and saw him staring down at her, his eyes shining bright with passion. She suctioned his length and loved how his lips parted to emit a hoarse cry. Faster she worked him, using a hand to cup and knead his balls as she dipped back and forth onto him.

"Pull back, I'm going to come," he panted.

She tightened her grip and pulled harder. His hips jerked and he cried her name when he came. The way he said it, so possessive sounding, sent a shiver through her frame. She took everything he had to give and swallowed it, basking in the moment. She even allowed herself to pretend he loved her.

Allowed herself to dream.

*

Solus was right about one thing, Fiona thought days later as their craft began its descent into the chosen planet's atmosphere. They did fight about her involvement in the operation to snag the human who'd hurt her. Fought, then had wild sex. Fought some more, and tore at each other's clothes. They battled with words, but neither would give way. She still wanted to kill the bastard. He wanted her safe.

The part of her that loved him, relished the fact he cared. The part of her that needed vengeance would not be swayed, no matter what he did to her body. And he did some truly pleasurable things in an attempt to change her mind.

The past few days had been glorious. While Solus still went about his duties, when his shift was done, he always knew where to find her. Sometimes they never even made it to the room, their coupling fast and furious where they stood.

The silly smile on her face seemed determined to not leave, especially since Solus, despite his words to the contrary, slept with her every rejuvenation period. Slept with her cradled in his arms, skin to skin.

Even Aramus, with his perpetual glower and snarled, "Get a room," couldn't put a damper on her happiness.

She would have foregone her vengeance possibly if it meant she could live that way forever.

However, the plan went on, and Einstein found a planet, a lush one that would serve them well. *And I will get my very first view of a true sky and vegetation.* Oddly enough, it made her tummy tighten and her pulse race.

What do I fear?

Analyzing her thoughts, she came to a lip tightening conclusion. *Once I step off this ship, everything will change.* Because once they'd accomplished their mission

138

and killed the humans, they would have no reason to stall any longer. Solus would take her to the cyborg planet, and the intimate bond they'd formed, the love she pretended existed between them would vanish as he returned to his life. His home. His world that had no place for a mate. No place for her.

*

Landed and ready to disembark, Fiona paused in the door way of the ship, as if fearful of stepping out. His hand gripped around hers, Solus stopped his descent on the gangplank and turned to regard her with a puzzled air.

"What's wrong? Are you scared?"

She nodded.

"But there is nothing to fear. I would never let anything harm you."

"I know you wouldn't." She sighed, then braced her shoulders before taking a hesitant step forward. She took a second and stopped. Her eyes widened. "The air," she whispered.

He took a big sniff and found nothing amiss. "What about it?"

"It has such strange smells. And yet my processor is not filtering them for toxins. What if they harm me?"

It took him a moment to realize the fragrance of the planet, with its lush foliage and flowers, made her uneasy. It brought all his protective instincts to the fore, and he drew her into his arms for a reassuring hug. "What you're scenting is the vegetation. Think of it as a perfume, an odor that is noticeable but not harmful and depending on the item emitting the scent, pleasant.

She gave a tentative sniff. "It is rather nice." She took a step, more hesitant now than when faced with anything else he'd seen her confront. It should have made him bark at her like he would a recruit. Instead, he found it endearing. He let go of her body to clasp her hand again, letting himself go at her speed.

With slow paces, she moved with him down the docking ramp, craning her head the entire time, her eyes shining with wonder. "The sky is a light purple."

"The ozone balance is not the same as earth's here, but the air ratio is close. Because this planet is not on any major shipping paths, the humans haven't yet decided to colonize it. We vetoed it as being too close. Besides, we found somewhere better."

"The cyborg planet is nicer?" She seemed to find that concept hard to grasp. He'd show her soon though. He actually looked forward to showing off the pristine world they'd claimed as their own. *And introducing her to my large and comfortable bed.* But first, he needed to put an end to the humans chasing Fiona, the bastards who'd dared hurt her.

An easy task compared to that of teaching her she could love. They'd not revisited the terms of their relationship since they started sleeping together. Solus actually feared bringing it up, unsure of how he would react if after the glorious days—and nights—they'd spent together, she continued to claim she didn't care for him. Could never love him. He, on the other hand, loved her all too much, and the feeling got stronger the more he learned about her. The more he touched her. It was the most wondrous and scary sensation all at the same time.

But not as frightening as knowing once their mission to terminate the humans was done, they'd go home. Once there, she expected them to go their separate ways. To live apart. Once the thing he thought he wanted most of all, now the thing he dreaded the most. How could he keep her with him? How could he make her see that she had it in her to love? *How do I make her love me?*

Maybe I'll just have to kidnap her again if she refuses to see reason. Take her away from the brethren to a place where we can be alone and I can convince her that while we are part machine, our

140

leftover humanity means we are capable of so much more. Capable of feeling. Of being together, forever.

Aramus's snorted. "Look at the pair of them, like moonstruck recruits. Makes me want a lobotomy I tell you," broke the loop Solus had fallen in.

It was Fiona's outstretched foot tripping the grumpy cyborg that made him laugh. A bristling Aramus picked himself up off the ground and raised a threatening fist.

Solus didn't need to act though, because Seth came bounding down the ramp with a taunting, "Hitting girls now are we? Is this because you can't beat a man?"

"She's cyborg," Aramus snapped.

Seth stopped in front of the bigger male and while his back was to Fiona, Solus clearly saw his expression. It was quite deadly.

"Listen here, dickhead. I might put up with your shit because I'm your friend, but even I draw a line somewhere. You don't hit women. Ever. I don't give a shit what they do to you. I don't care if they're as tough as you and can handle it. You ever raise your hand again to someone of the fairer sex and I'll rip it off and make you eat it." Seth smiled, but it wasn't an expression of mirth. "Are we clear?"

"Very. And while we're clearing the air, I am not your friend."

"Are too," Seth sang striding off into the jungle, Aramus close behind.

"Are not. So don't be telling people that you are, asshole."

"Make me."

Their bickering lasted several minutes as they went into the forested area exploring. Solus shook his head.

"Seth is a lot more dangerous than he seems, isn't he?" Fiona asked.

141

Not liking her noticing the younger male, Solus growled. "Kiss him again and you'll see who's more dangerous."

A smile tilted her lips. "Don't tempt me. It's a match I'd like to see."

Einstein joined them at that point, and they went to work, building a fake camp with the wood Aramus and Seth dragged from the jungle. They didn't need any fine finishing touches, just enough structure to make it look like a village from above. Well, except for one hut which he filled with soft fragrant boughs to serve as a bed. He and Fiona would sleep outside that night, free from the tight confines of the ship.

They made love under the stars, their brilliance casting a glow on her skin, making it gleam as he worshipped it. Its faint illumination was enough for him to see her expression when she came, screaming his name, clutching at his back. The moment was so perfect, so beautiful, he almost blurted it out. Almost said the dreaded, 'I love you,' managing to change it at the last minute to, "I love—I mean, I'd love it if you would just give me peace of mind and sit out the battle."

"But—"

"Please, Fiona. I promise to make the bastard hurt. Promise you will have your vengeance through me. But I need to know you're safe."

"Why?"

Why? Because he didn't think he could handle it if she were killed. Wasn't even sure he could handle it if she got injured. "As one of the few remaining cyborg females, it is my duty to make sure you are returned to the brethren uninjured. I would be remiss in my duties if I were to let you participate in a battle that could see you prematurely terminated."

Disappointment flooded her features. "I see. And of course, you always do your duty don't you?"

"It is the cyborg way."

A heavy sigh left her. "I will do as you ask." She then turned on her side, facing away from him.

For some reason, he felt like he'd done something wrong, he just couldn't figure out what. Solus lay down silently behind her. She didn't push him away when he spooned his body around hers, curling his arm around her waist.

Still, the tension in her body let him know she wasn't happy with him or her reluctantly given agreement.

Selfish or not, he didn't care. *At least she'll be safe.*

*

The body cradling hers relaxed and Solus's breathing came low and far apart, letting her know he'd fallen asleep. Fiona still bit her lip and locked her jaw, though, because the strange sensation that took hold of her at his cold reasoning for why she needed to hide away wouldn't ease. For a moment, she foolishly expected him to say he cared for her. That he couldn't bear to see her hurt. But no, instead, he spouted off some completely rational explanation for why she should abstain from the upcoming battle, and too tired to fight him anymore, she agreed. More like lied. Because no matter what he wanted, Fiona wouldn't sit idle while others fought her battle.

Despite her decision, she couldn't help feeling an odd hurt from his words. Nowhere in his speech did he claim he did it because he cared for her. She knew she shouldn't have expected him to. And yet....

Hot moisture pooled in her eyes. It was with shock, she recognized she cried real tears. What an awful external expression of her feelings. It made her chest tight, her throat close in and she put a fist in her mouth lest the sound beating inside her escape.

She would not show weakness. Would not give in to her human side. But the cool demeanor of her machine, no matter how she tried to access it, could not make the pain go away.

He doesn't love me. No matter how beautiful their time together had been. No matter how often they joined together in bliss, Solus didn't love her. And it hurt. Hurt worse than anything she'd ever known.

Chapter Twelve

Fiona woke the next day feeling refreshed and in a better frame of mind. In the light of day it was easier to remind herself that Solus only gave her exactly what he promised. His body, and nothing else. For her to foolishly hope it would turn into something more was a weakness instilled in her by her human psyche that she needed to overcome.

Work, as she'd discovered in the past, provided relief from her thoughts and emotions, and she threw herself into the tasks needed with enthusiasm. She pitched in with the others, learning to build using primitive means such as vine for ropes to bind limbs, and lashing fronds to form a roof. They taught her to build a fire, forage for food to keep them strong, and how to hunt the creatures that would harm them. Solus even taught her what it meant to garden, explaining how the plants grew and what stages they were in. There was something relaxing about having her fingers digging in the dirt, or stripping fruit from limbs. It kept her hands busy and her mind blank. It lasted until nightfall, when she let Solus fill her with pleasure, and she found contentment, even if tenebrous.

And so it went, day after day. They built, foraged and waited for the humans to arrive while tempers, actually only one in particular got short, at their inaction.

Aramus stomped around the camp, griping about everything from the bugs that harmlessly nipped at their skin to the long wait. He thought they should get back on their ship and proactively hunt down the military searching for her.

Outvoted by the rest, they instead remained where they were.

After their sixth day planet-side, running out of things to do, Fiona went for a walk to look for some of the sweet berries they'd discovered that were palatable. They'd exhausted the supply close to camp, so armed with a pistol, and with a wave to Seth, she went looking for more.

The peacefulness of the jungle eased a tension she'd not realized imbued her as she walked. The stress of keeping her secret love from Solus, while waiting for the humans to arrive, was taking its toll. She almost missed the days when the most she felt was fatigue after a hard day's work in the mine. But knowing what she did now, she still welcomed the stress because of how she felt for Solus.

She'd wandered for about fifteen minutes when she heard some grunting and fleshy smacks. It sounded like a fight, a sound she'd grown familiar with as the males tended to work out their stress in a physical manner. *I'll bet it's Solus and Aramus.* They'd wandered off earlier looking for more vines. It seemed they'd found another reason to spar instead—in other words, they worked on their frustration by hitting each other. Curious, she crept up to where she heard the sounds of fighting, until, crouched behind a large bush with just enough spacing between the foliage, she could spy. The sight stole her breath.

Both the males were shirtless, their trousers hanging low off their hips. While Aramus was made of big, bulky slabs of muscle, Solus was perfection with his slimmer muscled physique that lightly gleamed with sweat. His skin rippled as he moved, his body twining and lunging with a grace she never tired of.

It seemed they'd battled for a while already judging by the light bruising on their frames and their heavy pants as their body took in more oxygen to offset the strain of their muscles. Having a fresh air supply was a definite benefit she'd discovered, a boon that made her even stronger than before, her body flourishing with the constant stream of breathable gas.

Watching in the bushes, she smiled as she thought of what else flourished. A familiar moistness wetted her cleft as she watched Solus move with a smooth agility that never ceased to fascinate her. It roused a hunger that had nothing to do with the berries she'd initially left to hunt.

Perhaps she could waylay Solus after he and Aramus finished sparring. It wouldn't be the first time they copulated in the woods. As if he heard her wanton wish, the males stepped apart from each other, still glaring, their fists held tight to their sides.

"Are you done running your fucking mouth?" Solus asked in a tight, angry voice. "Or do I need to tenderize it some more?"

Rubbing his jaw, Aramus scowled. "I wouldn't have to say anything if you weren't being such a prick. You haven't exactly been acting rational lately."

"My functions are operating within normal parameters."

"Like fuck they are. Ever since you hooked up with that female, you've been inconsistent, letting your dick rule instead of logic."

"Jealous because I'm getting some?"

"No. Just waiting for you to go back to being a cyborg I can fucking look up to. You're no better than human now," Aramus said with a sneer. "Constantly at her beck and call. Hovering over her so she doesn't stub a toe. I never thought I'd see the day you let a woman own your balls. How the high and mighty Solus has tumbled."

"Not for long. Once we finish our operation and go back to our home planet, Fiona and I will be going our separate ways and I will go back to being the cyborg you once knew."

"I can't wait," Aramus replied. "It's been hell watching you play nursemaid to the female."

147

Fiona didn't wait to hear Solus agree. Tears running unchecked, she was already sprinting through the jungle, a frantic flight that caught at her clothes and hair, but she didn't stop, couldn't stop, not with his words ringing in her ears. *'…going our separate ways.'* She knew that moment was coming. Dreaded it. And yet, lying in his arms night after night, seeing his smiles and what seemed like unfeigned joy at her presence, she foolishly hoped that even if he couldn't love that they would at least continue as they were. Lovers with no strings, at least on his part.

His conversation to Aramus though laid that wistful dream to rest. And broke her heart.

Crushed by pain, she couldn't breathe. Couldn't think. She could only run away from the man who'd reminded her of her humanity, and made her wish she was only a machine.

She slammed into something during her flight, or more like was caught by something. She stared up into familiar eyes and groaned.

"Not you. Not now."

*

Aramus dared compare Solus to a nursemaid? "I am no one's nanny."

"Says the man who spends all his time with her."

"Because I happen to enjoy her company, dammit. Did that ever occur to you? And stop talking about her like she's weak," Solus snapped. "Fiona is strong. Brave. And yes, beautiful."

"So beautiful you're already planning your escape when we get home."

"Not by choice. I care for her, Aramus, and quite deeply, but I need to respect her wishes. She doesn't want a mate in her life. Doesn't think she's capable of love."

Aramus snorted. "Then why was she so upset?"

148

A frown creased his brow. "What are you talking about?"

"Don't tell me you didn't see your girlfriend over there spying on us? She ran off after she heard you saying you were going to split up when we get home."

Solus froze. "She was here?"

Aramus inclined his head and Solus looked behind him. He saw nothing, and almost turned back when he caught a glint. He strode several paces to the bush and plucked a golden strand from the branches. *She was here. But why did she leave?*

"What makes you think she ran off because of our conversation?"

"Oh she left because of it, crying her eyes out," Seth replied strolling into the clearing with a tight jaw. "What the hell is wrong with you?"

"With me," Solus demanded. "What the fuck are you talking about?"

Seth shook his head. "You're a fucking idiot. She overheard you telling Aramus that you were going to split up when you got home."

"Because that's what she wants."

"Is it? Have you asked her?"

"No. But it's what she said when she suggested we embark on a no-strings relationship. She has not said anything since to make me think she's changed her mind."

"You still haven't told her you love her, have you?"

"I don't have the capacity to love," he lied.

"Bullshit. You and Fiona are so god dammed stubborn. You love her. She loves you. And yet, instead of the pair of you admitting your feelings, you keep persisting in this charade that it's just about sex, and a little companionship. Meanwhile, you're both on pins and needles, so afraid of losing each other that you're making a ridiculous situation even worse."

149

"She loves me?" The very concept was like a punch to the gut, sucking all the air from his lungs.

"Well duh! Haven't you heard a word I've said?"

"She's never said it."

"Have you?"

Solus glared. "No."

"Why not?"

"Because he's afraid of looking weak. Afraid of rejection," Aramus said in a quiet tone.

Seth could have caught flies his jaw dropped so low. "My man, did you just say something meaningful? Quick, someone call Einstein. We need to send him in for a full diagnostic."

A familiar glower crossed the big cyborg's face. "Just because I don't approve of us having detrimental relationships doesn't mean I don't see what's going on."

"She told me she wasn't capable of love. That she didn't want me or anyone for a mate."

"And was this before or after you gave her the big speech on how you won't ever settle down and she'd be better off with someone else?"

Tight lips clamped shut was his reply.

"Exactly. So you told her that you had no room in your life for a woman. She still wanted your cold ass, so she told you what you needed to hear and now you're both too stupid to admit the truth."

"I don't like you," Solus stated.

"I don't like him either," Aramus replied. "I'll hold him down if you want to hit him."

"Now that you've agreed to form a club that dislikes me, can we get on with more important shit, such as the fact Fiona heard part of your conversation and thinks Solus is looking forward to dumping her? Or did it not occur to you that there is an unhappy cyborg female running around, by herself in the jungle while a cursed human ship is hiding behind the third moon?"

"The humans are here?"

Seth had the grace to look sheepish. "Yeah, that was kind of why I started following Fiona in the first place, to keep an eye on her, and tell you guys if I saw you because Einstein said we shouldn't use our wireless in case they can tap it."

"Have they landed any shuttles?"

"Uncertain. If they did, then Einstein missed it on his scans, but anything is possible with their new technology."

"Where did she go?"

Seth shrugged. "You should count yourself lucky I'm even telling you since she begged me to not say anything. But she can't have gone too far."

"You idiot. Why did you leave her alone? There's humans around."

"Maybe. Or did you miss the part where I said Einstein didn't detect any shuttles landing."

"I need to go after her," Solus said, grabbing his shirt from a pile on the ground and putting it on. He grabbed his heavy weapon belt, hung with a sword on one side and pistol on the other, and buckled it around his waist.

"Want us to come with you?"

"Since we're not sure where she is, we should fan out," Solus stated as he began to walk away from his friends. "Seth, you sweep around to the east, Aramus the west, I'll go straight north. If you find her, get her to the safe spot we designated." They'd built her a shelter in a tree, out of sight and with foliage dense enough to fool even the more precise scanners.

Jogging, he headed north, a specific destination in mind. With a sense born not of logic but an irrational feeling in his gut, he believed he knew where she hid. Or so he hoped.

No matter where you are, I'll find you, and tell you how I feel, because for once, Aramus is right. I am acting like a coward, and that is just not acceptable. I will tell you I love you, and if you don't feel the same, then I am going to fight to win your heart. Fight with everything I have because it is the cyborg way dammit! And you're worth the battle.

Chapter Thirteen

Initially, Fiona ran blindly, putting as much distance between herself and the other cyborgs as possible, her heart, unable to handle the pain, running the show. Branches whipped at her face and arms, tearing at her hair and clothing, not that she paid the minor damage any heed, not when her most grievous injury consumed her entirely. She didn't plan a course or destination, but it was with not too much surprise that she ended up at the cave.

My cave. The one Solus found for her. He'd discovered it during one of his hunting expeditions and brought her to it, a secretive smile on his lips. She'd walked with silent wonderment through the cavernous space, marveling at the brilliant striations on the rock which refracted with the slightest light. Delighted in the limestone-like stalagmites and stalactites that hung from the ceiling and projected from the floor, their textured rings showing their advanced age and cause for beauty.

The cave was beautiful and more importantly, special, because Solus found it and led her to it knowing she'd enjoy this touch of familiarity. On the floor of that wondrous place, he made her cry out in ecstasy, erotically torturing her until she squirmed and begged him to take her on a blanket he'd thoughtfully brought. A simple, woolen fabric that actually got a lot of use as they returned several times to be alone in her special place. A haven now tainted judging by the familiar blanket that lay rumpled on the middle of the cavern floor instead of neatly folded like she'd left it last.

Whirling, she was just in time to see a trio of humans blocking the cave entrance. All three brandished a weapon in her direction, and this close, they seemed unlikely to miss. She cursed, not for the first time, the emotional turmoil that deadened her usually sharp senses.

"Well, well," taunted the captain from the video. His face hid in shadow but his voice—she would never forget it. "If it isn't F814, the murdering, runaway droid. We've been looking for you."

And I've been waiting for you. She squared her shoulders. Cowardice was not an option. "I am not a droid. I am a cyborg and my name is Fiona, human."

He chuckled and suddenly, she couldn't help flashing back to the moment when he'd led the attack. Leering over her. Laughing as he held her down. Remembering might have frightened or weakened a lesser female, *but I am not an ordinary person.* The distasteful memories made her angry. Stronger. More determined. Made her almost gleeful, because despite Solus's wishes, it seemed she would have a chance at her vengeance. She just needed to get close enough.

As if sensing her train of thought, the captain waved his pistol. "Don't even think of firing that weapon of yours. It will go badly if you do. So unbuckle your belt with the holstered gun and drop it to the ground."

"And if I refuse?"

All the weapons steadied, aimed at her head. "We'll blow your cyborg brains out despite what the general wants."

With a tight smile, that made the captain's companions shift nervously, she took a step forward as her hands undid the buckle to her utility belt. "So, the general is still alive?"

"That old bastard is too ornery to die, and he's real anxious to get you back. Even sent us with some new fangled weapon that apparently might take you and any other cyborg we come across down without permanent harm. But, I don't like to rely on maybes myself. So I'll stick to the old fashioned way of stopping a cyborg; blast you enough to remove that head of yours and there will be nothing left to control the body."

She ignored the last part of his threat to focus on the more worrisome part. The humans owned a weapon specially made to halt her kind? She needed to know more so she could warn Solus and the others. After she killed the captain of course.

"So where's the rest of your troops?" she queried as she took another step forward. The captain held his position, but his two companions retreated, casting nervous looks at each other and their leader.

"Safe on the ship. See, the general only wants you. And while your cyborg buddies might have found the decoy beacon and foolishly kept it stationary in their camp, they missed the other one in your foot. That was my idea before we shipped you into hiding on that dirty asteroid. See, we knew if you ever got lost, someone would be looking for one transmitter. But two?" He smiled. "Seems like I was right since it led me right to you. But you were asking about my troops. Only a dozen of us came down to the surface. I figured that was enough to take your metal ass down. Maybe I'll even take a piece of it, just like the good old days back at the compound."

"Only a dozen? That seems foolish given the number of us running around, waiting for a chance to kill you," she replied, baring some teeth in her smile.

His sneer didn't waiver. "Ah yes, your new cyborgs pals. Yes, let's talk about them. See, at this very moment, my ship is arming its lasers and any moment now it's going to torch your cyborg village until all that's left is a crater of ash. Even machines can't survive that kind of inferno. But lucky you, you get to come with me. And did I mention, it's going to be a *long* voyage home?"

"You'll have to kill me, because I refuse to go anywhere with you," she said in a pleasant voice, amused that he'd fallen for their ruse. She had her doubts when they built the fake village.

He laughed. "And how do you figure on escaping?"

Ducking, quicker than the human eye could follow, she scooped a rock and threw it as she scuttled forward. It hit one of his men in the forehead before he could fire, dropping him to the ground. While it took care of the one soldier, it didn't stop the captain, or his other lackey, from opening up fire.

Dirt sprayed as the projectiles struck the ground at her feet. She bent her bionic knees and bounded straight up.

"Don't kill her you fucking idiot. The general wants her alive."

Landing several feet closer to the humans, she'd just wrapped her hand around another rock when lightning struck her. The familiar feel of electricity coursing through her system dropped her to the ground and her fingers loosened around her shard of stone.

Not again.

Blinking at the ground, her eyesight grew dim, and a roaring white noise muffled all sound. Despite all the licks she'd endured by the former overseer's electric whip, the energy surge was too much for her to handle. Paralyzed, she wanted to scream at the injustice of it all.

To have come so close to freedom only to lose it. To have seen some of the galaxy and yet so little. So many things to regret, and yet the one thing she regretted most was, *I found love and didn't have the courage to admit it.* And now she'd never have the chance, she thought as her eyes fluttered shut.

Chapter Fourteen

Solus move quickly through the jungle to the cave, and still arrived too late. Or just in time depending on how a being processed the situation.

The stupid humans—*who dare to think they can take my Fiona*—stood with their backs to the jungle, except for one who lay on the ground, his forehead a bloody mess. It seemed his female wasn't about to give in to their threats.

Solus crept with silent feet toward the remaining threat and held in his cry of rage when the captain—*the human who will die screaming*—pointed a taser inside the cavern. Solus well knew what the weapon could do.

Fiona!

The time for stealth passed. A metallic clarion rang as his sword cleared its sheath. A heartbeat later it plunged into soft flesh. With a scream of surprise, the corporal, who flanked Solus's true target, looked down. Solus could well imagine the view, not pleasant given the tip of his sword emerged from his chest.

Pulling back, the blade withdrew with a wet sucking sound and the body fell to the ground. In the same moment, the captain turned around and regarded him with a hatred Solus knew all too well.

Solus snarled. "Prepare to die, human."

"Move and the cyborg bitch gets it."

To Solus's surprise, the human didn't aim his weapon at him, but instead at Fiona's inert head. A fatal shot if fired.

His heart stopped. "What makes you think I care if you shoot?"

"Our scanners picked up two sets of fluids from the blanket you left behind in the cave. Hers and a males. I'd wager you're that male."

"And?"

"Are you really as cold as you want me to think?" the captain taunted. "Let's find out." He angled his wrist and shot Fiona in the thigh.

The leg twitched. Blood pooled and Solus roared as he lunged, stopping dead when the captain placed the barrel of his gun against her head.

"You won't leave this planet alive," Solus growled. "You've marked yourself for death."

An explosion in the distance made the ground rumble and a smirk crossed the human's face. "There goes your camp and reinforcements. Looks to me like your options are getting slimmer and slimmer, machine. I can't believe the general and his cronies are so scared of you. How many of you were there? A dozen? Two? Whatever the number, it's a lot smaller now."

"You seem to forget the ones that were out hunting. And the one before you."

"And you seem to forget who's in charge here, machine." The captain put pressure on the trigger and panic set in.

I can't watch her die. Not while I still live. "Take me instead," Solus offered. He let his sword slip to the ground and dropped to his knees, placing his hands on his head. "I will give myself up, without a fight, if you let the female go."

"What makes you think I want you? My orders were to fetch F814. Dead or alive."

"But imagine if instead you came back with a live male? Don't tell me your general wouldn't jump at the chance."

Incredulity marked the captain's face. "You'd give yourself up to save her?"

"I'd do anything for Fiona. So do we have a deal, human?"

"I don't negotiate with machines," the captain sneered raising his gun to point it at Solus's face.

"We are more than machines," Fiona yelled, rolling onto her back while scissoring her legs. She took down the human in a flurry of limbs. In the space of a heartbeat, she straddled the captain, his gun spinning uselessly off into the brush while her hands cupped his neck.

"Defective bitch. You won't get away with this. Now that your camp is gone, there's even fewer of you than before. We'll hunt you down and kill—"

Fiona squeezed as Solus came to stand behind her, then knelt to put a hand on her shoulder in support—and because he needed to reassure himself that she was alright.

"Surprise," she almost sang. "That camp is a decoy. The only thing you destroyed was a mirage. And the only thing dying is you." She increased the pressure of her fingers and watched in stony silence as the human clawed at her hands, his eyes bulging as he gasped for air. When his struggles grew weak, she spoke again, a soft whisper. "You won't be hurting me or anyone else, ever again." With a sharp twist, she broke his neck.

Solus gathered her into his arms and dragged her off the corpse, hugging her tight to him. "I thought I was going to lose you," he whispered against her hair, his voice tight, and his eyes prickling strangely.

Fiona pulled back to look him in the eye. "Why did you offer yourself to him? Why would you trade your life for mine?"

"Because…" The words clung to the tip of his tongue. Once spoken, they could never be returned. He could never go back to his solitary lifestyle. His cold, analytical persona. His lonely existence.

"I love you. I know it's illogical, and impractical, and a whole host of other unreasonable things, but I can't help it. I love you, Fiona, and I don't want us to be apart when we go home. I want you with me forever."

Her mouth hung open as she stared at him, shock in her eyes and face. The fear he'd come to hate, made his heart stutter.

A brilliant smile lit her face. "Oh, Solus. I love you too. I think I have from the moment you disarmed me in the tunnels."

Like an idiot, he just had to question. "But I thought you didn't think you could love?"

"I did. However, being with you taught me that I can love. I can live. I can be happy." She leaned forward until their foreheads touched and her lips hovered just out of reach. "But only if you're at my side."

She kissed him softly.

"I think I'm going to throw up some metallic parts," Aramus grumbled, his voice distinctive and unwelcome. Reining in a sigh of annoyance, Solus raised his head to see the big cyborg as he stepped from the forest, Seth at his side.

"About time you got here," Solus growled. "Fiona was almost killed."

"We ran into a few humans on the way. They were going to look at the hole they made. We gave them some new holes to worry about," Seth said with a grin.

"Where's Einstein?" Fiona asked. "Is he okay?"

A sudden explosion in the sky made them look up. A shower of burning parts rained across the horizon. It was almost pretty. *Fuck me, I am turning into Joe.* He'd get Seth to smack some sense into him later. First, he needed to check on his friend.

Solus opened his neural pathway. *"Einstein?"*

"Yes? Did you like the fireworks? I've been working on a new stationary weapon, a trap if you will, and I'm pleased to say it went off without a hitch."

"Glad to know you're safe, brother. I am shocked thought that the humans made it by you in the first place."

Solus could almost hear Einstein's growl. *"The humans used some kind of cloaking device I've never encountered. I didn't even note they were there until they dropped the shield for a moment, probably to launch a craft, which I might add I couldn't detect either."*

"That's not good."

"No kidding. The military seems to have gotten their hands on some new technology, and we'd better find a way to counter it fast or we could be in trouble."

"We'll tell Joe about it when we get back. He'll probably want to put together a team and go looking for it."

"I'll scan the jungle for the landing craft on my way to fetch you."

"Sounds good. We'll meet you at the rendezvous point."

He closed his communication portal. "He's fine," Solus said aloud. "He took out the military spacecraft, and will meet us at the riverhead."

"He would kill them all with his fancy technology," Aramus grouched as he stalked away, Seth at his side.

"Yeah, what a jerk, killing all those humans in one fell swoop and not saving any for us," Seth said turning his head long enough for them to see him rolling his eyes. "Don't worry, old friend. I'm sure we'll find a few stragglers on the way."

"Do you really think so?" Aramus asked in a hopeful lilt.

Fiona slapped a hand to her mouth but couldn't quite halt the giggle that emerged.

No force in the universe could have stopped him from hugging her to him and kissing her tempting lips. *She loves me.* And that was cause for celebration.

*

Fiona wanted to run a full diagnostic because surely she'd heard Solus wrong. *He said he loved me!* That he wanted her forever. Perhaps, the captain had killed her. Or she dreamed again while he shipped her inert body. The kind of joy she currently felt couldn't be real. Couldn't be possible.

Solus drew back from the embrace, his dark eyes searching her intently. "What's wrong?"

"I'm afraid this is just a dream. That I'll wake up and be back in my nightmare." A world without Solus.

"Never again, Fiona. I will never let the humans take you away from me. I will do everything in my power to make you happy. To make you smile and laugh like you deserve. I love you so much it frightens me, and yet, I wouldn't have it any other way."

Moisture pooled in her eyes and her words emerged as a tight whisper. "I love you, Solus. I never thought I'd understand what it meant, but I do. I need you. I would do anything for you so long as we can be together."

"Then let me love you. That's all I want or need." His lips almost bruised her as he took her mouth with a savage passion that she welcomed. Standing, pressed body to body, his arms hugging her, she met him kiss for kiss, moan for moan. And demanded more.

A fierce urgency imbued her. A desire, make that a fiery need, to have him inside her gripped her and thankfully, seemed to grip him too.

"I want you," he groaned against her mouth. He thrust his groin against her, the hardness of his cock evident, and welcome. "However, it's too dangerous. There could be more humans around."

"So protect me. Aren't you supposed to be a master at multitasking?" she asked with grin. "Surely you can pleasure me while keeping an eye out for danger. I need you inside me." she replied, her voicing turning husky.

"But your wound," he still protested as she slid her hands down his body to his waist. She quickly unfastened his trousers and slipped a hand inside, grabbing hold of his dick and stroking it. He groaned as she caressed him, reveling in the solidity of his erection, loving the hot smooth skin encasing it.

"My wound is already healing. I am cyborg, after all. I guess I'll have to convince you." She dropped to her knees, evading his hands and licked his swollen head, sucking him into her mouth, moisture pooling in her sex at his hoarse cry.

When she got him to a certain point, she released him long enough to say, "You're right. Maybe we should wait until we get back to the ship. We wouldn't want to get ambushed with your pants around your ankles."

He looked almost comical, looming over her, his mouth agape and his cock jutting. He grasped her hair, twining his fingers through it, and brought her back until her lips rubbed the tip of him. "Let them try and interrupt. It'll be the last thing they fucking do."

She laughed, a sound that rumbled along his length as she opened her mouth and took him back in. She sucked him fervently, bobbing her head, peeking up at him to see his jaw tight, but his eyes open as he scanned the woods. Multitasking, how cyborg of him. She clamped her teeth onto his skin and dragged them up his length and his whole body shook at the intensity. It also made him lose his concentration and she grinned to herself as his eyes closed for a moment, basking in the moment.

As if realizing his sudden inattention, he growled. "Naughty wench. I try to keep us safe and you're determined to distract me."

"Is it working?"

"Too well. So now it's time for a little payback. Come here." He beckoned her up and she stood, one hand clasped around his length still stroking. "Have I told you today how beautiful you are?"

She shook her head, sending blonde strands flying.

"I will add it to my daily tasks then so I don't forget," he said with a grin, stroking her lower lip with his thumb. He kissed her, a soft sensual tease that had her gasping. While he toyed with her mouth, his hands made quick work of the closure holding her pants together. A soft breeze kissed the bare skin of her buttocks when he pushed them down. He slid a hand between her thighs, touching her moist sex. She closed her eyes as she enjoyed his touch and moaned as he rubbed her clit.

"So beautiful," he murmured.

She opened her eyes to see him staring at her.

"I want you to bend over for me. Hold your ankles and watch the woods while I do to you what you did to me."

Fiona did as he asked, her eyes scanning the forest for movement, a task forgotten with the first slow lick of her sex.

He tortured her with his tongue, running it along the seam of her lips. Flicking it against her sensitive nub. Made her keen and pant as he dug his fingers into her thighs and set out to pleasuring her with a single mindedness she loved. He wouldn't let her climax, retreating every time she got close. She finally had to beg.

"Solus, please."

"Anything for you, Fiona," he said in a gruff voice.

She heard him stand behind her and the tip of him probed at her. She thrust back against him, no longer content to wait, impaling herself on his length. Oh, the exquisite feel of him. Stretching her. Filling her. Claiming her as his. In and out he pumped. His body slapped against hers. Driving. Deep. She ached. Bent over as she was, she could only moan, and enjoy as he controlled the pace, his rhythm quickening until he veritably pistoned her sex. And she loved it.

She screamed his name as she came, shuddering waves without end that milked his cock, and rolled into a second climax that made him dig his fingers deep as he found his own release.

"I love you," he shouted as he spilled inside her.

"Forever," she gasped.

"Forever," he agreed.

Which, given their part machine status could be a very long time, which suited her just fine.

Later on, cradled in his arms in their room on the ship, she reflected on her new life.

I used to dream I was a human. I lived a nightmare as a robot. But because of Solus's love and patience, I now know I am more than a machine. I am Fiona, and from this moment on, I decide the course of my life, and I choose to love.

Epilogue

Fiona strode down the gangplank, her hand firmly tucked in Solus's. After weeks in space, it was nice to finally get to their destination, the cyborg planet, even if it also terrified her. This was to be her new home. A real planet, with living vegetation, and water and a house. A house she'd share with Solus.

How would she adapt? What if she hated the planet? She'd rather enjoyed the one with the purple sky they visited for a short time. Could this one truly compare? How would Solus react to sharing his space? Would he change his mind? She knew she would she miss the intimacy she and Solus shared on the ship. What if…?

Her thought process trailed off as she beheld the cyborg world. "It's beautiful," she whispered.

Exotic, bright, and lush, while the space around their craft was cleared and covered in gravel, the rest of the scenery was a canvas of color, from the turquoise fluff on the ground, to the soaring trees with trunks striated black and grey, bearing foliage in a deep red. And the sky —

"It's blue!"

Solus laughed. "Yes, a little darker than the earth one, but that is the only resemblance to the colors you'll have seen in the videos, or that you remember. I will take you exploring once I've settled you into our home."

"Our home." She murmured the words. They seemed so strange still. Add to that she still worried about pushing Solus and she had to ask, "Are you sure?"

"About?"

"Sharing your house. I mean, I could always —"

He shut her up with a kiss. "You belong with me. I'll hunt you down if you try to stay anywhere else. I love you, Fiona. And I meant what I said about forever. Get used to it."

"Bossy machine. I love you too. But still, I heard how much your space means to you."

"And there's no one I'd rather share it with. Or my bed, which I might add is quite big," he said with a mischievous smile.

"I kind of liked our small one," she quipped.

He kissed her again, and it might have gone on for a while, had the sound of someone clearing their throat not separated them.

"Solus, old friend, I've got three words for you. Told you so."

Fiona laughed at the pained look on her lover's face. She turned to face the newcomer, noting his height and bright blue eyes. "You must be, Joe. I've heard many things about you," she said.

"It's nice to meet you, too. I heard a lot about you from my old friend here. I have to admit though, I never thought I'd ever meet someone brave enough to take on Solus as mate."

"Mate?" she queried.

"Mate," Solus stated firmly, wrapping an arm around her waist. "For now and always."

Before she could digest what he'd said, her attention got caught by a smaller figure behind Joe that stepped into view with a shy smile. She was quite pretty with her long dark hair, short stature and curvy figure.

"Hi, F814. Or should I say, Fiona? It's been a while."

"Chloe." Fiona breathed the name. Her heart tightened in her chest and moisture pooled in her eyes when the other woman nodded, her own eyes damp. Fiona wasn't sure how it happened but they ended up in each other's arms, hugging and crying. She, the female who once thought she was a droid, shedding tears of joy.

"Defective females," Aramus snorted as he went by.

Sniffing and laughing, Fiona pulled away from Chloe. Joe tucked the smaller female against his side, the soft smile he aimed down at her full of affection. She recognized that look because she saw it often on Solus's face.

Fiona looked around while wiping her damp cheeks and blurted out the first thing that came to mind. "Where's Bonnie?"

Chloe went still. "What did you say?"

"You must remember her? Bonnie, unit B785. You never went anywhere without her. I kind of figured you would have been found together. I guess I should have questioned Solus more." At Chloe's continued blank stare, Fiona frowned. "Surely if you remember me then you recall her. She is after all your biological sister."

Joe caught his fainting mate before she could answer, but Fiona had no such reprieve and found herself stuck amidst a flurry of questions.

She halted them by raising her hands, an act reinforced by Solus's growled, 'Stop it and give her a chance to speak."

Fiona shrugged her shoulders. "I'm sorry. I don't know much more than what I said. Heck, I didn't even remember most of it until I saw C791. Sorry, I mean Chloe. B785 is Chloe's sister. The military, for some reason, let them keep that knowledge, or at least they did for a while. I don't recall ever seeing one without the other."

The last time I remembered seeing them, they were holding each other tight, waving at me and my other sisters, tears spilling from their cheeks. Reassigned, if I recalled correctly, and even in the tight prison of my mind, bound by programming and torture, I hoped they went to a better place, somewhere the abuse might stop. As for me and the other females, it had just begun.

"Do you know where she might be?" Joe asked, while a tearful Chloe, now conscious again listened avidly.

Fiona shook her head, partially to disperse the flashback and also in answer. "Sorry. I didn't even realize I knew that much, but seeing Chloe again triggered a few memories."

"A sister," Chloe murmured. "Oh God. How could I have forgotten?"

"I think it goes without saying," Joe replied, standing with his mate cradled in his arms. "That we will do our utmost to find her."

"And bring her back to you," Seth said solemnly.

"After we kill the pricks who have her," Aramus added. "Get the ship fueled and someone to replace loverboy, Solus, over here. I need a mission to get me out of here before all these womanly tears make my machine parts rust up."

"One day, Aramus," Joe said. "You're going to meet your feminine match, and when you do…"

"You'll never be the same. And I'll even wager you'll smile," Solus added.

"Never!" Aramus exclaimed.

But a cyborg knew better than to declare an absolute. And Fiona couldn't wait to see the big guy fall.

First though, she and her mate had a bed to baptize, and a whole world to discover. It turned out better than any dream.

*

The flames in the metal barrel rose higher, the dry documents being hand fed to the fire fanning it into a pyre. Ash swirled around as a gust of wind scooted past, snagging a ripped portion of paper, its edges charred, the writing smudged in many spots, but not enough to obscure the big red stamp that said 'DESTROY.'

Classified

[a whole section of the document is blackened out, obscuring it]

Project: Cybernetic X Factor

Unit: B785 [the writing is smudged with soot]

Attributes: [Another section blacked out, several paragraphs worth]

Notes: 05/09/2043 Since the separation from unit C791, B785 is nonresponsive to training or commands despite repeated attempts. ~~Termination recommended.~~ 05/30/2043 Unit reassigned to vessel SS Gunfrey bound for the outer colonies. Update: 07/05/2043 Unit lost during skirmish with galactic pirates. File slated for destruction.

The End (of this story)

Stayed tuned for Book 3 of *Cyborgs: More Than Machines,*

B785.

Author Biography

So you want to know a little about me? Well, I'm in my later thirties, married eleven years to a wonderful, supportive man—yes, he's a hunk—who gave me three beautiful, noisy children aged ten, seven, and five. I work as a webmistress and customer service rep from home, and in my spare time—of which there is tragically too little—I write, read, or Wii.

I was born in British Columbia, but being a military brat lived a little bit everywhere—Quebec, New Brunswick, Labrador, Virginia (USA), and finally Ontario. My family and I recently relocated to the Ottawa area to be closer to family and now that we're here, I'm sure they'll be putting the 'For Sale' sign up on their lawns soon lol.

Wow, was that ever boring! Now for the fun stuff.

I'm writing romance the way I like it—hot with a touch of humor and spice. I tend to have a lot of sexual tension in my tales as I think all torrid love affairs start with a tingle in our tummies. My heroes are very male; you could even say borderline chest thumping at times, but they all have one thing in common; an everlasting love and devotion to their woman.

Visit me on the Web for news on current and upcoming releases at

http://www.EveLanglais.com

Thanks for reading.

More Books by Eve Langlais
Published by Amira Press:
Alien Mate, Alien Mate 2, Alien Mate 3
Broomstick Breakdown
Dating Cupid
Defying Pack Law (Pack Book 1)
Betraying The Pack (Pack Book 2)
Taming Her Wolf
His Teddy Bear
Scared of Spiders
The Hunter (Realm series)

Published by Liquid Silver Books:
Lucifer's Daughter (Princess of Hell Book 1)
Snowballs In Hell (Princess of Hell Book 2)
Hell's Revenge (Princess of Hell Book 3)
Crazy
Date With Death
Hybrid Misfit
Last Minion Standing
Toxic
Wickedest Witch

Published by Cobblestone Press:
A Ghostly Ménage
Apocalypse Cowboy
Cleopatra's Men
Fire and Ice
My Secretary Series (BDSM shorts)

Published by Champagne Books:
Chance's Game (Realm series)
Take A Chance (Realm series)

Published by Eve Langlais
The Geek Job
Bunny And The Bear (Furry United Coalition Book 1)
Swan And The Bear (Furry United Coalition Book 2)
Delicate Freakn' Flower (Freakn' Shifters Book 1)
Jealous And Freakn' (Freakn' Shifters Book 2)
Accidental Abduction (Alien Abduction Book 1)
Intentional Abduction (Alien Abduction Book 2)
Dual Abduction (Alien Abduction Book 3)
C791 (Cyborgs: More Than Machines Book 1)

2829915R00091

Printed in Great Britain
by Amazon.co.uk, Ltd.,
Marston Gate.